WHEN ANYTHING CAN HAPPEN, WHO CARES WHAT HAPPENS?

Truly, there is not much bumpier or more boring reading than fantasy and science fiction in which the primal power of those fields has been harnessed to no deeper purpose than "patching potholes." No fear of that when Poul and Karen Anderson team up! Oh there is magic here in plenty, but the literary discipline is iron-hard, and the logic is as sharp as whetted elven steel . . .

What is it that the Vintners buy that is half so precious as the stuff they sell? Find out in

THE UNICORN TRADE

THE UNICORN TRADE
BY POUL AND
KAREN ANDERSON

A TOM DOHERTY ASSOCIATES BOOK

THE UNICORN TRADE

This is a work of fiction. All the characters and events portrayed in this book are fictional, and any resemblance to real people or incidents is purely coincidental.

A TOR Book

Published by:

Tom Doherty Associates, Inc.
8-10 West 36th Street
New York, New York 10018

First TOR printing, April 1984

ISBN: 812-53-085-3
Can. Ed.: 812-53-086-1

Cover art by: Tom Kidd

Printed in the United States of America

ACKNOWLEDGMENTS

Our thanks to Dr. Ralph Solecki of Columbia University for permission to quote the abstract of an article by him in *Science*.

Previously published material is originally copyrighted as follows:

"The Unicorn Trade," The Magazine of Fantasy and Science Fiction, April 1971, © 1971 by Mercury Press, Inc.

"Ballade of an Artificial Satellite," The Magazine of Fantasy and Science Fiction, October 1958, © 1958 by Mercury Press, Inc.

"The Innocent Arrival" (under the title "The Innocent at Large"), Galaxy Science Fiction, July 1958, © 1958 by Galaxy Publishing Company.

"Six Haiku," The Magazine of Fantasy and Science Fiction, July 1962, © 1962 by Mercury Press, Inc.

"Think of a Man," Galaxy Science Fiction, June 1965, © 1965 by Galaxy Publishing Company.

"Dead Phone," The Saint Mystery Magazine, December 1964, © 1965 by Fiction Publishing Company.

"The Kitten," *Frights*, © 1976 by Kirby McCauley.

"Planh on the Death of Willy Ley," SFWA Forum, August 1969, © 1969 by Science Fiction Writers of America.

"Murphy's Hall," *Infinity Two*, © 1971 by Lancer Books, Inc.

"Single Jeopardy," Alfred Hitchcock's Mystery Magazine, October 1958, © 1958 by H.S.D. Publications, Inc.

"In Memoriam: Henry Kuttner," The Magazine of Fantasy and Science Fiction, May 1958, © 1958 by Mercury Press, Inc.

"A Feast for the Gods," The Magazine of Fantasy and Science Fiction, November 1971, © 1971 by Mercury Press, Inc.

"Theoretical Progress" and "Investigation of Galactic Ethnology," The Magazine of Fantasy and Science Fiction, September 1964, © 1964 by Mercury Press, Inc.

"Look Up," The Magazine of Fantasy and Science Fiction, February 1965, © 1965 by Mercury Press, Inc.

"The Sky of Space," The Magazine of Fantasy and Science Fiction, March 1963, © 1963 by Mercury Press, Inc.

To
John and Bjo Trimble

THE UNICORN TRADE

They graze at night, the unicorns, upon the
   fresh-dewed grasses,
     Molten starlight flying as they toss their
     sapphire horns,
They step with light and dainty hoof below
   the stony passes,
     Shimmer under shadow where the night-
     ingale mourns.
       The bright manes ripple over dapple
       flanks,
       Quarter-moon racing past cloudy banks—
Now on the warning wind of dawn they flee
   night's crimson death;
They sleep in velvet forest shade; they spice
   it with their breath.

The castle queens it on her hill, the crown
   of pride and power,
     Turreted and traceried and carven like a
     gem,
With sunny court and golden hall, with wall
   and lordly tower
     Rich-tapestried with vine and grape, with
     rose on thorny stem;
       Rubies, damask, pomanders and swords—
       Wild loves, black hates, delights of wine
       and words—

Let pipe and tabor play! and thus, hand
   resting light on hand,
With quicker-beating heart we'll foot the
   skipping allemande.

There's goodly trade in unicorns, in castles
   and their treasure,
   Dragons are much demanded, endless
     caverns, eagly crags,
There's trade in rings of elven work, in songs
   of striding measure,
   Star-smiting curses, aye, and quests, and
     splendid thumping brags.
     Come buy, come choose your heart's
      desire of these,
     Fable and dream, wondrous commodities.
Already yours, these unicorns, as aught you
   owned yestre'en,
This castle, real as memory, that none but
   you have seen.

               —KAREN ANDERSON

FAIRY GOLD

Women, weather, and wizardry are alike in this, that their beneficences are apt to be as astonishing as their betrayals.

—The Aphorisms of Rhoene

It is an old tale, often told: a young man loved a young woman, and she him, but they quarreled, whereupon he went off in search of desperate adventure while she wept in solitude. However, this time it was not quite so. Arvel stormed down Hammerhead Street toward the Drum and Trumpet, where he intended to get drunk. Lona, after a few angry tears, uttered many curses and then returned to her pottery, where she punished the clay with her fists and pedaled the wheel until it shrieked.

The hour being scarcely past noon, Arvel found none of his cronies in the tavern, only a half-dozen sailors. Trade had grown listless throughout Caronne, after much of the kingdom's treasure bled away abroad during the Dynasts' War. Ships that came to Seilles often lay docked for weeks before their masters had sold all cargo. The markets at Croy were a little better, but the Tauran League now held a monopoly of them.

These men were off a vessel that had arrived on the morning's tide. They sat together, drinking like walruses rescued from a desert, rumbling mirth and brags, pawing at the wench whenever she came to refill a goblet. Arvel recognized the language of Norren, though he did not speak it. A couple of them were not of that land, but dark-hued, while the manes and beards of the rest were sun-bleached nearly white and their skins turned to red leather. Evidently they had been in the tropics.

Worldfarers! His longing took Arvel by the throat. He flung himself down at a table in a corner, hard enough to bruise his bottom. A sunbeam struck through a window leaded together out of stained glass scraps, to shatter in rainbows on the scarred wood. Smoke and kitchen smells lapped around him.

The wench came through the gloom, her clogs loud on the floor. "Joy to you," she greeted. Surprise caught her. "Why, Arvel, what a thundercloud in your face. Did a ghost dog bite you today?"

"A pack of them, and the Huntsman himself to egg them on," he snarled. "Wine—the cheapest, because I'll want a plenty."

She fetched, took his coin, and settled on the

bench opposite. Pity dwelt in her voice and countenance. "It's about your girl, isn't it?" she asked low.

He gave her a startled blue glance. "How can you tell?"

"Why, everyone knows you're mad with your wish to go oversea, and never a hope. But that's had you adrift by day, not at drink before evening. Something new must have gone awry to bring you in here so early, and what could it be save what touches your betrothal?"

Arvel swallowed a draught. Sourness burned its way down his gullet. "You're shrewd, Ynis," he mumbled. "Yes, we're done with each other, Lona Grancy and I."

The wench looked long at him. "I never thought her a fool," she said.

Despite his misery, Arvel preened a trifle. He was, after all, quite young, and various women had assured him he was handsome—tall, wide-shouldered, lithe, with straight features, slightly freckle-dusted, framed by fiery hair that curled past his earrings. As a scion of a noble family, albeit of the lowest rank, he was entitled to bear a sword and generally did, along with his knife; both were of the finest steel and their handles silver-chased. Otherwise, though, he perforce went shabby these days. The saffron of his shirt was faded and its lace frayed, his hose were darned, the leather of jerkin and shoes showed wear, the cloak he had folded beside him was of a cut no longer modish.

"Well," he said, after a more reasonable gulp of wine than his first, "she wanted to make a potter of me. A potter! Told me I must scuttle my dream, settle down, learn a—" he snorted— "an honest trade—"

"And cease being a parasite," Ynis finished sharply.

Arvel jerked where he sat, flushed, and rapped in answer: "I've never taken more than is my right."

"Aye, your allowance. Which is meager, for the bastard son of a house that the war ruined. What use your courtliness any more, Arvel Tarabine, or your horsemanship, swordsmanship, woodsmanship?"

"I guide—"

"Indeed. You garner an argent here and there, taking out parties of fat merchants and rich foreigners who like to pretend they're born to the chase. If they stand you drink afterward, you'll brag of what you did in the war, and sing 'em a song or two. And always you babble about Sir Falcovan and that expedition he's getting up. Is this how you'll spend the rest of your years, till you're too old and sodden for it and slump into beggary? No, your Lona is not a fool. You are, who wouldn't listen to her."

He stiffened. "You get above yourself."

Ynis eased and smiled. "I get motherly, I do." She was plump, not uncomely but beginning to fade, a widow who had three children to nurture and, maybe, a dream or two of her own. "You're a good fellow, mauger your folly, and besides, I like your girl. Go back, make amends—"

"*Hej, pige!*" bawled a Norrener from across

the taproom, so loudly that a mouse fled along a rafter. *"Mer vin!"*

Ynis sighed, rose, and went to serve him. She had been about to quench the rage that her words had refuelled in Arvel. Now it flamed up afresh. He could not endure to sit still. He tossed off his drink, surged from the bench, and went out the door, banging it shut behind him.

To Lona came Jans Orliand, chronicler at the Scholarium of Seilles and friend of her late father. This was not as strange as it might seem, for Jans was of humble birth himself and had married a cousin of the potter. Afterward he prospered modestly through his talents, without turning aloof from old acquaintances, until the hard times struck him too.

Lona had just put a fresh charge of charcoal under her kiln and pumped it akindle with the bellows. She was returning to her wheel when his gaunt form shadowed the entrance. She kept the shed open while she worked, even in winter, lest heat and fumes overcome her; and this was an amiable summer day. Nevertheless she had a healthy smell about her, of the sweat that dampened her smock. A smudge went across her snub nose. A kerchief covered most of her gold-brown hair.

"Joy to you," Jans hailed. He paused, to squint nearsightedly at her small, sturdy frame and into her green-brown eyes, until he said: "Methinks you've need of the reality, not the mere ritual."

"Is it that plain to see?" she wondered. "Well—

whoops!" In an expansive gesture, he had almost thrown a sleeve of his robe around one of the completed vessels that lined her shelves. She stopped him before he sent it acrash to the floor. "Here, sit down, do." She offered him a stool. "How may I please you, good sir?"

"Oh, let us not be formal," he urged, while he folded his height downward. She perched on the workbench and swung her feet in unladylike wise; but then, she was an artisan, in what was considered a man's occupation. "I require cups, dishes, pots of attractive style; and you, no doubt, will be glad of the sale."

Lona nodded, with less eagerness than she would ordinarily have felt. Feeling his gaze searching her yet, she forced herself to tease: "What, have you broken that much? And why have you not sent your maidservant or your son?"

"I felt I had better choose the articles myself," Jans explained. "See you, I have decided on renting out the new house, but its bareness has seemed to repel what few prospective tenants have appeared."

"The new house?"

"Have you forgotten? Ah, well, it was years ago. My wife and I bought it, thinking we would move thither as soon as we could sell the old one. But the war came, and her death, and these lean days. I can no longer afford the staff so large a place would demand, only my single housekeeper. The taxes on it are a vampire drain, and no one who wants it can afford to buy it. I've posted my offer on every market board and had it cried aloud through every street—without result. So at last my hopes are reduced to becoming a landlord."

"Oh, yes, I do recall. Let's pick you out something pretty, then."

Still Lona could not muster any sparkle. Jans stroked his bald pate. "What hurts you, my dear?" he asked in a most gentle tone.

She snapped after air. "You . . . may as well hear . . . now. Soon it will be common knowledge. Arvel and I . . . have parted."

"What? But this is terrible. How? Why?"

"He—he *will* not be sensible. He cannot confess . . . to himself . . . that Sir Falcovan Roncitar's fleet is going to sail beyond the sunset without him—" Lona fought her wish to weep, or to smash something. She stared at her fingers, where they wrestled in her lap. "When that happens . . . I dread what may become of him. We could, could survive together . . . in this trade . . . and today I told him we must . . . b-because the father of my children shall not be a drunken idler—And he—O-o-oh!" She turned her wail into an oath and ended bleakly: "I wish him luck. He'll need it."

In his awkward fashion, Jans went to her and patted her shoulder. "Poor lass, you've never fared on a smooth road, have you?" he murmured. "A child when you lost your mother; and your father perforce made you his helper; and when he too wended hence, there was no better inheritance for you than this."

Lona lifted her head. "It's not a bad little shop. It keeps me alive. It could keep a family."

Jans winced. She saw, and welcomed the chance to escape from herself. "What pains you?" she demanded. "It's your turn for telling."

He stood aside from her. His back sagged, while a sad little smile tugged his lips upward. "Oh, an irony," he replied. "The single form of humor the gods know, I believe."

"I don't understand."

"Quite simple, 'tis. Hark." He confronted her. "When for a time it appeared that Arvel might indeed sail off to the New Lands, and you with him as his bride, were you not also ablaze? Be honest; we speak in confidence."

"Well—" She swallowed. "Not in his way. I would have been sorry to forsake this my home for a wilderness. Nonetheless, I was ready to go for his sake, even if I must sell out at a great loss. And in truth, I would have welcomed such a chance to better ourselves and bequeath a good life to our children." She spread her empty hands. "Of course, I knew from the first it was likeliest a will-o'-the-wisp. He would have had to borrow the sum required, and where, without security? His father's estate entailed. Nobody who might desire this shop and cottage is able to pay a reasonable price, wherefore they are just as unmortgageable. After he tried, and failed, I besought him to settle down here and at least earn a steady living; but there it was I who failed."

Jans raised a finger to hush her. "No matter that," he said. "My first point has been made. Id est, imprimis, you would have left these premises if you could.

"Secundus, the dowries for my daughters exhausted my savings, and nature has not outfitted my son for my own sort of career. You know Denn Orliand for a good lad, and good with his hands, who at present toils as a day laborer, for miserable wages, whenever he can find work. I could buy him a shop of some kind, as it might be this very one, were my small capital not trapped by that incubus of a second house."

"We're all trapped," Lona whispered.

"Tertius," the dry voice marched on, "I looked forward to your wedding, for I am fond of you and Arvel is by no means a bad fellow. I had a book for a gift, a geography which migrants to the New Lands should find helpful or at least amusing, as the case may be, and which is in any event a sumptuous volume—"

"Jans." She took his nearer hand in both of hers.

"Quartus," he ended, "you might have had occasion to send me a wedding gift from oversea in your turn."

"What?" she exclaimed.

He glanced away and cleared his throat. "Um-m . . . a lady in reduced circumstances, forced to work in a tavern—but a fine person. As a matter of fact, I met her when Arvel once took me to the, m-m, Drum and Trumpet."

"Ynis!" Lona trilled. "Why, I've met her myself a time or two, but I never suspected—"

"Well, but of course I cannot think of assuming any fresh obligation before I have provided for the last child that my Iraine gave me, namely, Denn. The, m-hm, the lady in question agrees."

"Does Denn?" Scorn tinged her voice.

"Oh, he has no idea of all this," Jans answered hastily. "Pray do keep silence about it. And bear in mind, too, that . . . Ynis . . . would be most unwise to give up her present position, distasteful though it often is to her, and marry an aging widower, unless her stepson is able to provide for her and her children if necessary. Denn is loyal, he would do so, but he must have a foundation for his own life before he can, must he not? We are being sensible, even as you are."

Lona swallowed again. "Yes." She jumped down from the bench. "Come," she said, around an uncertain smile, "let's choose your things."

Natan Sandana the jeweler was visiting Vardrai of Syr the courtesan. The occasion was not the usual one. The small gray man had always contented himself with his wife, rather than spend money on the favors of other women, especially when they were as expensive as Vardrai's. His desire was for a different sort of joining.

"I tell you, we cannot lose," he urged, while he paced excitedly back and forth. The rug drank down every footfall. "My guild maintains a farflung web of communication—which stays healthy, sick though business has otherwise become. I had word of that Norrener ship soon after she had sailed from Owaio. Scarcely was she moored at the Longline this morning but I was aboard, to speak with her captain and look into his strongbox. The news was true. Besides

his cargo of spices and rare woods, he has, for himself, such a store of pearls as I never saw aforetime. White, rosy, black, all huge, all perfect, oh, I have today let Beauty's embodied being trickle through these fingers!"

"How did he get them?" asked Vardrai from the couch whereon she had curled her magnificent body. She continued to stroke a comb through the mahogany sheen of her tresses.

Natan shrugged. "He did not say. But it's known that while they were down among yon islands, the Norreners ·lent their aid—ship, cannon, pikes—in a war between two kinglets, for hire. I conjecture that the good Haako picked up some booty about which he did not inform his royal employer."

"And he'd fain sell the lot?"

"What else? He can get a substantial price at home. However, he understands it will be but a fraction of the true value. If we, here, outbid it, we shall still have a fantastic bargain."

Vardrai set the comb down and touched the necklace that her throat graced. "Pearls are fine to wear," she observed, "but who can eat them? If you can scarcely move what stock you have in your shop, Master Sandana, how can you realize a profit on such a hoard?"

"Some can be sold quickly," he maintained. "Not everyone·suffers in this abominable climate of trade. Zulio Pandric, for example, waxes fat, and nowadays is my best customer."

She grimaced the least bit. "And mine, or one of them," she murmured, half to herself. "I wish I could charge some less than others. A lusty young man would make up for a bloated old moneylender. But he and his kind seem to have all the gold, and I dare not risk word leaking out that Vardrai of Syr can be had cheaply."

"For the most part, the pearls will have to be held for several years, perhaps as much as a decade, until conditions improve," Natan admitted. "But conditions will. They must. If nothing else, once Sir Falcovan Roncitar has established his colony overseas, the wealth of the New Lands will begin flowing back to Caronne, and we know with certainty how lavish the gods were when they fashioned that part of the world. Gems will not only command their present rightful price, they will have appreciated enormously. Think, my lady. How would you like a profit of two or three hundred per centum?"

The woman sighed. Her glance strayed to an open window which, from this upper floor, overlooked King's Newmarket. The breeze that blew in was soft and quiet, for little of the olden bustle stirred on the square; dwindled were the very odors of foodstalls and horse droppings. Cultivated musicality slipped from her voice as she said, in the provincial accent of her childhood, "The trick is to stay alive till then. How much do you need?"

"I bargained him down to four hundred aureates—"

Vardrai whistled.

"—of which I can provide half, if I pledge sufficient property to Master Pandric," Natan said. "But we must be swift. Unlike so many merchant skippers, Haako expects to sell his cargo at a brisk rate, to wholesalers as well as the rich and the noble. Then he'll be off."

The jeweler halted before Vardrai's couch. "My lady," he pleaded, "I came to you because your trade is still faring well, and it is general knowledge that you are not extravagant, but put money aside. What say you to a partnership, share and share alike?"

Slowly, she shook her lovely head. "I say wonderful—but impossible," she told him with regret. "I have not the likes of such cash, nor could I leave it with you to ripen for ten years or so if I did."

"But," he protested. "But."

"I know." She gestured at those velvet hangings, ivory-inlaid furnishings, crystal chandeliers, fragrant incense burners which decorated the room. She ran a palm down the thin silk which draped her in luster. "I command high prices, because the alternative is to be poor, miserable, and abused down in Docktown or along the canals. But this means my gentlemen are not many. It also means that they expect this sort of environs, and much else that is costly; and it must be often changed, lest they weary of sameness. No, it's true that large monies pass through my hands, but what remains is scant, hard though I pinch. Besides, as I said, I cannot wait ten years."

"Why not?"

Vardrai turned her left cheek toward the window and pointed to the corner of that deep-violet eye. A sunbeam, slanting over a roof opposite, brought forth the tiny crow's-feet as shadows. "I am less young than you may think," she said quietly. "Time gnaws. I have seen what becomes of old whores."

Despite his disappointment, Natan felt a tinge of compassion. "What will you do?"

She smiled. "Why, I hope within that decade to have collected the wherewithal to buy a house and start an establishment wherein several girls work, paying commissions to me. That will give me my security and . . . and freedom."

Her gaze went outward again, fell on a red-haired youth who was crossing the marketplace with furious long strides, and followed him. A madam could have whatever lovers she chose, requiring no more of them than that they please her.

A gong sounded. "Come in," Vardrai called. A maidservant opened the door and announced: "My lady, there's a patron. Somebody new."

"Indeed?" Interest quickened the courtesan's tone. "Who?"

"He's a Norrener, my lady, but seems quite decent. Says he's the captain of a ship."

Natan chuckled, a trifle bitterly. "Ah, ha!" he remarked. "I expect you'll find Haako Gray-fellsson rather a change from Zulio Pandric."

"Let me hope so," Vardrai replied. "Well, go back, Jayinn, and entertain him while I make ready. I fear you must leave now, Master Sandana; and I *am* sorry I couldn't help you."

Over the cobblestones, between high, half-timbered walls, through arcades, beneath over-

hangs, across the plazas and a bridge spanning
the Imperial Canal, Arvel Tarabine stalked.
Almost, he ran. Passersby whom he jostled would
begin to curse, espy the fury on his brow and
the white knuckles on his fists, and keep silent.
A couple of wagoners halted their mules to let
him by, as if otherwise he would have cut a way
for himself. Dogs barked at him, but from a safe
distance.

Truth to tell, he fled his rage and grief, lest
they cause him indeed to harm someone; but
they rode along with him, inside his breast.
They kicked his heart, squeezed his lungs, clam-
bered about on his rib cage, and mouthed at
him. Perhaps, he thought, he could exorcise them
by wearing his body down to exhaustion—but
how much liefer would he have gotten into a
fight!

Out the Eastport he went, and soon left Tholis
Way for a trail northward. Seilles had long since
outgrown its old defensive walls, but not far in
that direction, because there the land climbed
steeply, in cliff and crag and ravine. Not even
shepherds cared to make use of it, nor did
noblemen risk breaking their horses' legs in the
chase. Peasants sometimes went afoot after deer,
or set snares for birds and rabbits—yet seldom,
for wolves prowled these reaches and, it was
whispered, beings more uncanny than that.

The trail was merely a track winding up hill-
sides and along ridges, often overgrown by whins.
Strong though he was, after two hours of it
Arvel must stop to catch his breath. He looked
about him.

Stillness and warmth pressed down out of a sky where no clouds were, only a hawk whose wings shone burnished. The air had a scorched smell. Gorse and scrub trees grew around strewn boulders, save where the heights plunged sheer. Afar and below was a forest canopy, richly green, and beyond it the Ilwen estuary gleamed like a drawn blade. He could just discern the city, walls, towers, ruddy-tiled roofs, temple spire, Scholarium dome, Hall of Worthies and palace of the Lord Mayor, warehouses and a couple of ships at the Longline, all tiny at this distance and not quite real. It was as if Lona were a dear dream from which he had been shaken awake.

His glance traveled westward. The sun cast a blaze off the rim of the world yonder—the bay, and behind it the ocean. Despair lifted over-whelmingly in him. That dream was also lost. Everything was lost.

How he had implored Sir Falcovan! "I proved myself a good fighting man in the war, one who can lead other men, did I not? Your colony may well need defenders. It will certainly need explorers, surveyors, hunters, and you know I can handle such matters too. As for a regular business, well, I'd be ill at ease on a plantation, but the trade in timber, furs, gold, ores—Take me, my lord!"

The great adventurer twirled his mustachios. "Most gladly, son," he answered, "if you can outfit yourself and engage whatever underlings you require, as well as help pay our mutual costs. Two hundred and fifty aureates is the price of a share in the enterprise. The Company cannot take less, not in justice to those who've already bought in. And you'll need another hundred or so for your own expenses."

That much money would keep a family in comfort for some years, or buy a large house or a small shop here at home. "My lord, I—I'll have to borrow."

"Against prospective earnings?" Sir Falcovan raised his brows. "Well, you can try. But don't dawdle. The ships have begun loading at Croy. We must sail before autumn."

"My . . . my wife, the wife I'll have, she's strong and willing the same as I," Arvel begged. "We've talked about it. We'll go indentured if we can't find the money." Lona had resisted that idea violently before she gave in, and he misliked it himself, but passage to the New Lands, to a reborn hope for the future, would be worth seven years of bondage.

The knight shook his head. "No, we've no dearth of such help—nigh more than we can find use for, to be frank. It's capital we still need: that, and qualities of leadership." His weathered visage softened. "I understand your feelings, lad. I was your age once. May the gods smile on you."

They had not done so.

Abruptly Arvel could no longer stand in place. He spun about on his heel and resumed his flight.

The weariness that he sought, he won after a few more hours. He staggered up Cromlech Hill and flopped to the ground, his back against the warm side of a megalith. A forgotten tribe had raised this circle on the brow of this tor, unknown millennia ago, and practiced their rites, whatever those were, at the altar in the middle. Now the pillars stood alone, gray, worn, lichenous, in grass that the waning summer had turned to hay, and held their stony memories to themselves. People shunned them. Arvel cared nothing. He thought that he'd welcome a bogle or a werewolf, anything he could rightfully kill.

The heat, the redolence, a drowsy buzzing of insects, all entered him. He slept.

Chill awakened him. He sat up with a gasp and saw that the sun was down. Deep blue in the west, where the evenstar glowed lamplike, heaven darkened to purple overhead. It lightened again in the east, ahead of a full moon that would shortly rise, but murk already laired among the megaliths.

"Good fortune, mortal." The voice, male, sang rather than spoke.

Arvel gaped. The form that loomed before him was tall, and huge slanty eyes caught what luminance there was and gave it back as the eyes of a cat do. Otherwise it was indistinct, more than this dimness could reasonably have caused. He thought he saw a cloak, its flaring collar suggestive of bat wings, and silvery hair around a narrow face; but he could not be sure.

He scrambled to his feet. "Joy to you, sir," he said in haste while he stepped backward, hand on sword. His heart, that would have exulted to meet an avowed enemy, rattled, and his gullet tightened.

Yet the stranger made no threatening move, but remained as quiet in the dusk as the cromlech. "Have no fear of *me*, Arvel Tarabine," he enjoined. "Right welcome you are."

The man wet his lips. "You have the advantage of me, sir," he croaked. "I do not think I have had the pleasure of meeting you erenow."

"No; for who remembers those who came to their cradles by night and drew runes in the air above them?" A fluid shrug. "Names are for mortals and for gods, not for the Fair Folk. But call me Irrendal if you wish."

Arvel stiffened. His pulse roared in his ears. "No! Can't be!"

Laughter purled. "Ah, you think Irrendal and his elves are mere figures in nursery tales? Well, you have forgotten this too; but know afresh, from me, that the culture of children is older than history and the lore which its tales preserve goes very deep."

Arvel gathered nerve. "Forgive me, sir, but I have simply your word for that."

"Granted. Nor will I offer you immediate evidence, because it must needs be of a nature harmful to you." The other paused. "However," he proposed slowly, "if you will follow me, you shall perceive evidence enough, aye, and receive it, too."

"Why—what, what—?—" stammered Arvel. He felt giddy. The evenstar danced in his vision, above the stranger's head.

Graveness responded: "You are perhaps he for whom the elvenfolk have yearned, working what poor small magics are ours in these iron centuries, in hopes that the time-flow would guide him hither. You can perhaps release us from misery. Take heed: the enterprise is perilous. You could be killed, and the kites and foxes pick your bones." A second quicksilver laugh. "Ah, what difference between them and the worms? We believe you can prevail, else I would not have appeared to you. And if you do, we will grant you your heart's desire."

There being no clear and present menace to him, a measure of calm descended upon Arvel. Beneath it, excitement thrummed. "What would you of me?" he asked with care.

"Twelve years and a twelvemonth ago," related he who used the name Irrendal, "an ogre came into these parts. We think hunger drove him from the North, after men had cleared and plowed his forest. For him, our country is well-nigh as barren; unicorn, lindworm, jack-o'-dance, all such game has become rare. Thus he turned on us, not only our orchards and livestock but our very selves. Male and female elf has he seized and devoured. Worse, he has taken of our all too few and precious children. His strength is monstrous: gates has he torn from their hinges, walls has he battered down, and entered ravening. Warriors who sought him out never came back, save when he has thrown a gnawed skull into a camp of ours while his guffaws rolled like thunder in the dark. Spells have we cast, but they touched him no deeper than would a springtime rain. To the gods have we appealed, but they answered not and we wonder if those philosophers may be right who declare that the gods are withdrawing from a world where, ever more, men exalt Reason. Sure it is that the Fair Folk must abide, or perish, in whatever countrysides they have been the tutelaries; we cannot flee. Hushed are our mirth and music. O mortal, save us!"

A tingle went along Arvel's backbone. The hair stirred on his head. "Why do you suppose I can do aught, when you are helpless?" he forced forth.

"For the same reason that the ogre has not troubled your race," Irrendal told him. "You have powers denied those of the Halfworld— power to be abroad by daylight and to wield cold iron. Uha, so named by the Northerners, knows better than to provoke a human hunt after him. We elves have already tried to get aid from men, but too much iron is in their homes, we cannot go near; and in these wilds we found none but stray peasants, who fled in terror at first sight of one like me. You do not. Moreover, you are a fighting man, and bear steel."

His voice rang: "Follow me to Uha's lair. Slay him. You shall have glory among us, and the richest of rewards."

"Unless he slays me," Arvel demurred.

"Aye, that could happen." Scorn flickered. "If you are afraid, I will not detain you further. Go back to your safe little life."

The rage, that had smoldered low in the man, flared anew, high and white-hot. An ogre? Had he, Arvel, not wished for something to attack? "Have done!" he shouted. "Let's away!"

"Oh, wonder of wonders," Irrendal exulted. And the moon rose.

Its radiance dimmed the stars that were blinking forth, turned grass and gorse hoar, frosted the starkness of stones. It did not make the elf any more clear in the man's sight. "Follow me, follow me," Irrendal called and slipped off, shadow-silent.

Arvel came after. He saw well enough by the icy light to trot without stumbling; but the hillscape seemed unreal, a mirage through which he passed. Only his footfalls and smoke-white breath made any sound. The chill grew ever deeper. Now and then he thought he glimpsed strangenesses flitting by, but they were never there when he looked closer.

Once Irrendal showed him a spring, where he quenched his thirst, and once a silvery tree whereon glowed golden fruit; he ate thereof, and an intoxicating sweetness removed all hunger from him. Otherwise he followed his half-seen guide while the moon climbed higher and the constellations trekked westward. The time seemed endless and the time seemed like naught until he came to the cave of the ogre.

It yawned jagged-edged in a cliff, like a mouth full of rotten teeth. Despite the cold, a graveyard stench billowed from it, to make Arvel gag. The bones, tatters of clothing, bronze trappings that lay scattered around declared that Irrendal had spoken truth.

Or had he? Sudden doubt assailed Arvel. Fragmentary recollections of the nursery tales floated up into his mind. Did they not say the elves were a tricksy lot, light-willed and double-tongued, whose choicest jape was to outwit a mortal? Was it not the case that nothing of theirs could have enduring value to a man? Irrendal had promised Arvel his heart's desire, but what might that actually prove to be?

Doubt became dread. Arvel was on the point of bolting. Then Irrendal winded a horn he had brought forth from somewhere, and it was too late. Cruelly beautiful, the notes were a challenge and a mockery; and they had no echoes, even as the bugler had no shadow.

Hu-hu, hu-hu, attend your doom!

The ogre appeared in the cave mouth. Monstrous he was, broad and thick as a horse, taller than a man despite a stoop that brought his knuckles near the ground. Eyes like a swine's glittered beneath a shelf of brow, above noseless nostrils and a jaw where fangs sprouted. The moon grizzled his coarse pelt. Earth quivered to each shambling step he took. Hatred rumbled from his throat as he saw the elf, and he gathered himself to charge.

"Draw blade, man, or die!" Irrendal cried.

Arvel's weapon snaked forth. Moonlight poured along it. Fear fled before battle joy. His left hand took his knife, and thus armed, he advanced.

The ogre grew aware of him, bawled dismay, and sought to scuttle off. Faster on his feet, Arvel barred escape, forced his enemy back against the cliff, and sprang in for the kill.

Uha was as brave as any cornered beast. An

arm swept in an arc that would have smeared Arvel's brains over the talons had it made connection. The human barely skipped aside. He had accomplished only a shallow slash of sword. But where the steel had been, ogre-flesh charred and smoked.

Uha lumbered after him. Arvel bounded in and out. His sword whistled. When a hand clutched close, he seared it with his knife. Uha bellowed, clattered his teeth, flailed and kicked. Irrendal stood apart, impassive.

The fight lasted long. Afterward Arvel recalled but little of it. Finally Uha won back into his den. The man pursued—altogether recklessly, for in there he was blind. Yet that was where the nightmare combat ended.

Arvel reeled out, fell prone upon the blessed sane earth, and let darkness whirl over him.

He regained strength after some while, sat painfully up, and beheld Irrendal. "You have conquered, you have freed us," the elf sang. "Hero, go home."

"Will . . . we meet . . . again?" Arvel mumbled with mummy-parched tongue.

"Indeed we shall, a single time," Irrendal vowed, "for have I not promised you reward? Await me tomorrow dusk beneath the Dragon Tower. Meanwhile—" he paused—"leave your steel that slew the ogre, for henceforth it is unlucky."

The thought passed through Arvel's exhaustion that thus far his pay was the loss of two good, costly blades. However, he dared not disobey.

"Farewell, warrior," Irrendal bade him, "until next twilight," and was gone.

Slowly, Arvel observed that the moon had passed its height. Before the western ridges hid it from him, he had best be in familiar territory; nor did he wish to linger *here* another minute.

He crawled to his feet and limped away.

Entering Seilles at dawn, he sought the sleazy lodging house where he had a room, fell into bed, and slept until late afternoon. Having cleansed off grime and dried sweat with a sponge and a basin of cold water, and having donned fresh albeit threadbare garments, he proceeded to the Drum and Trumpet, benched himself, and called for bread, meat, and ale.

Ynis regarded him closely. "You seem awearied," she remarked. "What's happened?"

"You'd not believe it if I told you," he answered, "nor would I."

In truth, he was unsure whether he remembered more than a wild dream on Cromlech Hill. Nothing spoke for its reality save aches, bruises, and the absence of his edged metal. The loss of Lona was more comprehensible, and hurt worse.

Eating and drinking, he wondered if his wits had left him. That was a thought to shudder at, madness. But life as a hale man would be dreary at best. What could he do?

Not creep back to Lona, whine for forgiveness, and seek to become a potter. She would despise him for that, after the hard words he had uttered yesterday, as much as he would himself. Besides, he'd never make a worthwhile partner in the shop. His hands lacked the deftness of hers and his tongue the unction of a seller—not that she ever truckled to anybody.

If he stayed on in Seilles, he had no prospect other than a continuation of his present miserable, cadging existence. Opportunities elsewhere—for instance, going to sea—were niggardly. But at least he would be making his own way in the world.

As he had wished to do, and been sure he could do magnificently, in the New Lands. Well-a-day, how many mortals ever win to their heart's desire?

Arvel sat bolt upright. Ale splashed from the goblet in his grasp.

"What is it that's wrong, dearie?" Ynis asked.

"Nothing . . . or everything. . . . I know not," he muttered.

The sun had gone behind the houses across the street. Soon it would go behind the horizon. Irrendal had said to meet him at the Dragon Tower.

What was there to lose? Simply time, if last night's business had been delirium after all, and time was a burden on Arvel.

Granted, legend maintained that the elves were a shifty folk, and their powers among men weak and evanescent. He must not let any hopes fly upward. But did it do harm if his blood surged and he forgot his pains?

Swallowing the last of his meal, Arvel hastened out. "Farewell," Ynis called. He did not hear. Sighing, she moved toward a tableful of rowdies who whooped for service.

Hemmed in by walls, the streets were already dark, but people moved about. Linkmen were lighting the great lamps on their iron standards, while windows and shopfronts came aglow. Since the advent of modern illumination in Caronne, city dwellers kept late hours. Even those who had no work to do or money to spend enjoyed strolling and staring in the coolth of day's end. Arvel could understand why creatures of night and magic now avoided the homes of men.

Sunset chimes pealed from the temple as he passed Hardan's Port. It no longer existed save as a name; cannon had crumbled it and its whole section of wall during the Baronial War, and nobody felt a restoration was worth undertaking. Instead, the then Lord Mayor had turned the area into a public park. Trees that he planted on the borders had since grown tall enough to screen off view of surrounding mansions. Only the highest spires of the city pierced heaven above their shadowiness. Gravel scrunched under Arvel's feet, along labyrinthine flowerbeds. Their perfumes were faint at this eventide hour. A nightingale chanted through the bell-tones and fireflies wavered in air. No lovers had arrived, which struck him as odd.

At the center of a greensward reared that remnent of the old fortifications known as the Dragon Tower. Ivy entwined it, and the fierce heads carven under the battlements were weathered into shapelessness. Here an elf might well venture. Arvel's pulse fluttered. He took stance at the doorway. The chimes fell silent. The gloaming deepened. Stars trembled into view.

"Greeting, friend." Whence had the vague tall shape come? Arvel felt after the sword he no longer wore.

Laughter winged around him. "Be at ease," Irrendal sang. "You've naught to fear but folly."

Arvel felt himself redden.

"Against that, no sorcery prevails, nor the gods themselves," Irrendal continued. With the weight of the ogre off it, his slightly wicked merriment danced free. "Nor can the Halfworld ever be more in men's lives than transient, a sparkle, a breeze, a snowflake, a handful of autumn leaves blowing past. Still . . . much may be done with very little, if cunning suffices.

"I pledged to you your heart's desire, Arvel Tarabine. You must choose what that is. I can but hope you choose aright. I think, though, this should cover the price. Hold out your hand."

Dazedly, the man did. A gesture flickered. A weight dropped. Almost, in his surprise, he let the thing fall, before he closed fingers upon it.

"A coin of some value as men reckon value," Irrendal declared. "Spend it wisely—but swiftly, this same night, lest your newly won luck go aglimmer."

Was there a least hint of wistfulness in the melody? "Fare you well, always well, over the sea and beyond," Irrendal bade him. "Remember me. Tell your children and ask them to tell theirs, that elvenkind not be forgotten. Farewell, farewell."

And he was gone.

Long did Arvel stand alone, upbearing the heaviness in his hand, while his thoughts surged to and fro. At last he departed.

A street lamp glared where the city began. He stopped to look at what he held. Yellow brilliance sheened. He caught his breath, and again stood mute and moveless for a space. Then, suddenly, he ran.

Zulio Pandric the banker sat late at his desk, going through an account book which was not for anyone else's eyes, least of all those of the king's tax assessors. Lantern globes shone right, left, and above, to brighten the work, massive furniture, walnut wainscot, his gross corpulence and ivory-rimmed spectacles. From time to time he reached into a porcelain bowl for a sweetmeat. Incense made the air equally sticky.

To him entered the butler, who said with diffidence, "Sir, a young man demands immediate audience. I told him to apply tomorrow during your regular hours, but he was most insistent. Shall I have the watchman expel him?"

"Um," grunted Zulio. "Did he give you his name?"

"Yes, sir, of course I obtained that. Arvel Tarabine. He does not seem prosperous, sir, nor is his manner dignified."

"Arvel Tarabine. Hm." Zulio rubbed a jowl while he searched through his excellent memory.

"Ah, yes. A byblow of Torric, Landholder Merlinhurst. Father impoverished, barely able to maintain the estate. Son, I hear, a wastrel. . . . Admit him." Zulio had long pondered how me might lay such families under obligation. Here, conceivably, was a weak spot in the independence of one of them.

Eagerness made the fellow who entered as vivid as his flame-red hair. "I've a marvel to show you, Master Pandric, a whopping marvel!" he declaimed.

"Indeed? Be seated, pray." The moneylender waved at a chair. "What is this matter that cannot wait until morning?"

"Behold," said Arvel. He did not sit but, instead, leaned over the desk. From beneath his cloak he took a thing that thudded when he slapped it down.

Zulio barely suppressed an exclamation of his own. It was a gold coin that gleamed before him—but such a coin, as broad as his palm and as thick as his thumb. In a cautious movement, he laid hold on it and hefted. The weight was easily five pounds avoirdupois, belike more; and the metal was pure, he felt its softness give beneath his thumbnail.

A sense of the eerie crept along his nerves. "How did you come by this, young sir?" he asked low.

"Honestly." Arvel jittered from foot to foot.

"What do you wish of me?"

"Why, that you change it into ordinary pieces of money. It's far too large for my use."

"Let us see, let us see." Zulio puffed out of his chair and across the room to a sideboard. Thereon stood scales of several sizes, a graduated glass vessel half full of water, an arithmetical reckoner, and certain reference works. He needed no more than a pair of minutes to verify the genuineness of the gold and establish its exact value at those present rates of exchange which scarcity had created—four hundred aureates.

He brought the coin closer to a lantern and squinted. The lettering upon it was of no alphabet he knew, and he had seen many. The obverse bore a portrait of someone crowned who was not quite human, the reverse a gryphon.

Abruptly he knew what he held. Chill shivered through his blubber. He turned about, stared at Arvel, and said, each word falling like lead down a shot tower: "This is fairy gold."

"Well—" The youth reached a decision. "Yes, it is. I did a service for the elves, and it is my reward. There's naught unlawful about that, is there? I'd simply liefer the tale not be noised abroad. Too many people have an unreasoning dread of the Fair Folk."

"As well one might, considering their notorious deviousness. Don't you know—" Zulio checked himself. "May I ask why this haste to be rid of it?"

"I told you. I cannot spend it as it is. You can find a buyer, or have it melted into bullion, and none will suspect you of robbery as they could perchance suspect me. Chiefly, though, I want to travel. This will buy me a share in Sir Falcovan Roncitar's enterprise, and whatever else I'll need to win my fortune in the New Lands."

"Could you not at least wait until morning?"

"No. I was counselled—well, I know nothing about these matters, only that he warned me I'd lose my luck if I didn't act at once—and I do want to leave. Come morning I'll buy a horse and a new sword and be off to Croy, out of this wretched town forever!"

Zulio decided Arvel was honest. He really had no idea of the curious property of fairy gold. His impatience might be due to something as trivial as a love affair gone awry.

Yes, probe that. "No farewells, no sweetheart?" Zulio asked slyly.

Arvel whitened, flushed, and whitened. "She never wants to see me again—What's that to you, you fat toad? Break my coin and take your commission, or I'll find another banker."

"I fear—" Zulio began, and stopped.

"What?" Arvel demanded.

Zulio had changed his mind. He did not need to explain the situation. He would be extravagantly foolish to do so.

"I fear," he said, ignoring the insult, "that I shall have to charge you more than the usual brokerage fee. As you yourself realize, a coin so valuable, and alien to boot, is not easily exchanged. It will take time. It will require paperwork, to stave off the royal revenue collectors. Meanwhile the money I give you is earning no interest for me, and I must purchase additional precautions against theft—"

Arvel proved to be even less versed in finance and bargaining than Zulio had hoped. The banker got the elven piece for three hundred and fifty aureates, paid over in gold and silver of ordinary denominations while the watchman witnessed the proceedings.

"Help the gentleman carry these bags back to his lodgings, Darron," Zulio ordered courteously. "As for you, Master Tarabine, let me wish you every success and happiness in your New Lands. Should you find you have banking needs, the house of Pandric is at your service."

"Thank you," Arvel snapped. "Goodnight. Goodbye." Somehow, the immense adventure before him had not brought joy into his eyes. He lifted his part of the money easily enough, but walked out as if he were under a heavy burden.

Scarcely were the two men gone when Zulio stuffed the coin into a satchel and waddled forth to Crystal Street by himself. He could realize a large profit this night, but only this night. If he waited until dawn, his loss would be vast.

He did not think that Natan Sandana the jeweler, whose family and associates had been city-bred for generations, had heard anything about fairy gold. Quite probably Sandana did not believe the Halfworld was more than a nursery tale. Zulio came of backwoods peasant stock, and had dabbled in magic—without result, save that he acquired much arcane lore. Panting, sweating, he elbowed onward through crowds, amidst their babble and the plangencies of beggar musicians, underneath walls and galleries and lamp-flare, until he reached the home he wanted.

Natan was at his fireside, reading aloud from an old book—the verses of wayward Cappen Varra, which this prudent, wizened modern man loved—to his wife and younger children. He did not like or trust Zulio Pandric, and received his guest with an ill grace. Nevertheless, manners demanded that he take the banker into a private room as requested, and have the maidservant bring mulled wine.

Candles in antique silver holders threw mild light over bookshelves and paintings. The leather of his chair creaked beneath Natan as he leaned back, bridged his fingertips, and inquired the visitor's wishes.

"This is an irregular hour, yes," Zulio admitted. "I'd not ordinarily trouble you now. But the circumstances tonight are special. You are a man of discretion, Master Sandana; you will understand if I spare you long and tedious explanations. Suffice it that I have urgent need of gemstones, and do not wish to risk it becoming a subject of gossip."

Natan grinned. Zulio knew, annoyed, that he was thinking of the courtesan Vardrai. Well, what did his sniggers count for? He'd assuredly forget them in the morning. "I have therefore taken a rare coin, a virtual ingot, from my vaults and brought it hither," Zulio said. "Observe. Let us talk."

Discussion occupied an hour. Natan Sandana was not so rude to a prominent man of affairs that he tested the gold himself . . . then. He did ask for, and get, a certification of value. In return, Zulio accepted a receipt for payment in full. "Have a care," he warned, as he put four hundred aureates' worth of the finest diamonds into his satchel—or better, because the jeweler had been still more anxious to deal than the slack market warranted. "Some evilly gifted thieves have been at work of late, I hear. Rumor goes that they employ actual witchcraft. That is why my attestation explicitly disavows responsibility for any effects of sorcery, as well as mundane malfeasance. You could open your strongbox and find nothing but a pile of rubbish, left as a jeer at you."

"I thank you, but I doubt it will happen, and not just because I equate the supernatural with superstition," the other man replied. A feverish intensity had come upon him. Zulio wondered why.

No matter. He had his profit, a clear fifty aureates above what he had paid out to Arvel Tarabine, in the form of gems negotiable piecemeal. Puffing, chuckling, jiggling, Zulio Pandric hastened back to his ledger and his sweetmeats.

"I must go out, dear," Natan Sandana told his wife. "Don't wait up for me."

"What has happened?" she asked.

"An unbelievable stroke of luck, I hope," he said, and kissed her fondly. "I'll tell you later, if all goes well."

As he stepped forth, the coin in his pouch dragged at his belt. He felt as if every passing glance lingered on the bulge, and pulled his cloak around it. Should he have waited for morning, when he could engage a guard? But that would have been to make conspicuous a transaction best kept secret. Tax collectors were as rapacious as any unofficial robber.

Besides, who would think that a drably clad little gray man carried a fortune on his person? Especially nowadays, when that fortune had been languishing for years in stock he could not sell.

Natan took Serpentine Street, the best-lit and safest way through Docktown, to the Longline. There he must pass a number of empty berths before he reached *Sea Mule.*

Fore and aft, the castles of the Norrener carrack loomed darkling. Between them, her guns glimmered dully by the light of wharf lamps and lanterns of the watch on board; her three masts stood gaunt athwart a lately risen moon. Its glade trembled on the river, which murmured with currents and tide. Rigging creaked as hemp contracted in the night's damp chill.

"Oh-hoa!" Natan called. "Lower the gangplank. I've business with your captain."

The pikemen obliged, which relieved him. Haako Grayfellsson might have been ashore carousing. Instead, the big man slumped in his cabin, amidst the malodor of bear-tallow candles, and swigged from a bottle of rum.

"Well met, Master Sandana," he said in accented Caronnean and a tone which all but added, "I suppose."

"I'm happy to find you here," Natan said.

Haako stroked his red, barbaric beard. "You wouldn't have, if I'd not blown over-much money on a vixen I'd heard praised—Enough. What would you of me?"

Natan laid palms on the table and leaned across it. "No need to pussyfoot," he said. "About our conversation the day before yesterday. I am prepared to buy your pearls at the price we mentioned."

An oath blasted from Haako's lips, but it was a sound of utter delight. Briefly, Natan recalled Vardrai. Poor woman; in a way it was a shame how she had missed her chance at this investment. Well, so much the more for those whom he held dear.

"Why, welcome again," the courtesan purred. She undulated into a position where light shone through her shift and outlined every curve against a nighted window.

This time her pleasure and seductiveness were sincere. The Norrener seaman was a little uncouth, true, but he possessed a vigor which he used with some skill. She had been sorry when he told her that he could not afford a second visit.

He stood awkwardly in the scented room, twisting between his fingers a fur pouch that contained something round. Through the windowpane drifted a vibrancy of violin and flute. Vardrai made it worth those beggar musicians' while to keep station below this wall.

"I . . . have a . . . proposition for you," he mumbled. Strange how he blushed, like a virginal boy, this man who had dared hurricanes and spears.

"Oh, I *like* propositions." Vardrai drew close to him and ruffled his whiskers.

He seized her and kissed her. She seldom wanted a kiss on the mouth, but found that this time it was different. "What a woman you are," he groaned.

"Thank you, kind sir," she laughed, and fluttered her lashes at him. "Shall we try if that be true?"

"A moment, I beg you." Haako stepped back and took her by the shoulders. His callouses scratched her slightly, arousingly, as he shivered. Otherwise he was gentle. His eyes sought hers. "Vardrai, I—I've come into a chunk of money. Left to myself, I'll drink and dice it away, and soon have nothing for you . . . and my ship will be calling two or three times yearly in Seilles hereafter, it will." The words tumbled from him. "Here's my proposition. What say I give you the sum, right this now, in pure gold— and you let me see you free of charge, always after, whenever I'm in port? Is that a fair offer, I ask you? Oh, Vardrai, Vardrai—"

Wariness congealed her. "What sum do you speak of?" she asked.

"I've the coin right here, and a paper from banker Pandric to give the worth," he blurted, while he fumbled in his pouch. "Four hundred aureates, 'tis."

Her world swooped around her. She stumbled against him. He upheld her. "Four hundred aureates!" she whispered.

The moon sank west. Streets were deserted, save for the Lord Mayor's patrols, or peasants carting their produce to market, or less identifiable persons. The sounds of their passage rang hollow beneath the stars. Hither and yon, though, windows were coming to life with lamplight.

One belonged to the kitchen of Jans Orliand. Having slept poorly ever since he lost his wife, the chronicler was often up this early. He sat with a dish of porridge he had cooked for himself and read a book as he ate.

A knock on the door lifted his attention. Surprised, slightly apprehensive, he went to unlatch it. If that was a robber, he could shout and rouse his son Denn—but it was a woman who slipped through, and when she removed her hooded cloak, she was seen to be glorious.

"Vardrai of Syr!" Jans exclaimed. They had never met, but she was too famous for him not to recognize when they chanced to pass each other in the open. "Why, why, what brings you? Sit down, do, let me brew some herbal tea—"

"I have heard it cried that you've a house for sale, a large one with many rooms," she said.

He looked closer at her. Cosmetics did not altogether hide the darknesses below her eyes, or the pallor of cheeks and lips. She must have lain sleepless hour after hour, thinking about this, until she could wait no longer.

"Well, well, yes, I do," he replied. "Not that I expected—"

The wish exploded from her: "Could you show it to me? Immediately? If it suits, I can buy it on the instant."

Lona Grancy had also slept ill. The moon had not yet gone behind western roofs, and the east showed just the faintest silver, when she trudged from cottage to shed, lighted its lamps, and commenced work. "May as well," she said. "Not that customers will crowd our place, eh?"—this to her cat, which returned a wise green gaze before addressing itself to the saucer of milk she set forth.

The maiden pummeled clay, threw it upon the turntable, sat down, and spun the wheel with more ferocity than needful. It shrilled and groaned. She shivered in the cold which crept out from between her arrayed wares. The hour before dawn is the loneliest of all.

A man came in off the street. "Master Orland!" she hailed him. "What on earth?" The spinning died away.

"I thought . . . I hoped I might find you awake," the scholar said. Breath smoked ragged with each word. "I am pushing matters, true, but—well, every moment's delay is a moment additional before I can seek out a, a certain lady and—Could we talk, my dear?"

"Of course, old friend." Lona rose. "Let me put this stuff aside and clean my hands, then I'll fetch us a bite of food and—But what do you want?"

"Your property," said Jans. "I can give you an excellent price."

Again by herself, for her visitor had staggered off to his bed, Lona stood in her home and looked down at the coin. It covered her hand; its weight felt like the weight of the world; strange glimmers and glistens rippled across the profile upon it. Silence pressed inward. Wicks guttered low.

So, she thought, now she had sold everything. Jans would not force her to leave unduly fast, but leave she must. Why had she done it—and in such haste, too?

Well, four hundred aureates was no mean sum of cash. No longer was she bound to the shop which had bound her father to itself. She could fare elsewhere, to opportunities in Croy, for example; or, of course, this was a dowry which could buy her a desirable match. Yes, a good, steady younger son of a nobleman or merchant, who would make cautious investments and—

"And hell take him!" she screamed, grabbed the coin to her, and fled.

Arvel tried for a long while to sleep. Finally he lost patience, dressed in the dark, and fumbled his way downstairs. Lamps still burned along the street, but their glow was pale underneath a sinking moon and lightening sky, pale as the last stars. Dew shimmered on cobbles. Shadows made mysterious the carvings upon timbers, the arcades and alleys around him.

He would go to the farmers' market, he decided, break his fast, and search for a horse. When that was done, the shops would be open wherein he could obtain the rest of his equipage. By noon he could be on the road to Croy and his destiny. The prospect was oddly desolate.

However, no doubt he would meet another girl somewhere, and—

A small, sturdy figure rounded a corner, stopped for an instant, and sped toward him. "Oh, Arvel!" Echoes gave back Lona's cry, over and over. Light went liquid across the disc she carried. "See what I have for you! Our passage to the New Lands!"

"But—but how in creation did you get hold of that?" he called. Bewilderment rocked him. "And I thought you—you and I—"

"I've sold out!" she jubilated as she ran. "We can go!"

She caromed against him, and he wasted no further time upon thought.

When they came up for air, he mumbled, "I already have the price of our migration, dear darling. But that you should offer me this, out of your love, why, that's worth more than, than all the rest of the world, and heaven thrown in."

She crowed for joy and nestled close. Again he gathered her to him. In her left hand, behind his shoulder, she gripped the fairy gold. The sun came over a rooftop, and smote. Suddenly she held nothing. A few dead leaves blew away upon the dawn breeze, with a sound like dry laughter.

—Poul Anderson

BALLADE
OF AN ARTIFICIAL SATELLITE

Thence they sailed far to the southward along the land, and came to a ness; the land lay upon the right; there were long and sandy strands. They rowed to land, and found there upon the ness the keel of a ship, and called the place Keelness, and the strands they called Wonderstrands for it took long to sail by them.

  —Thorfinn Karlsefni's voyage to Vinland,
   as related in the saga of Erik the Red

One inland summer I walked through rye,
a wind at my heels that smelled of rain
and harried white clouds through a whistling
 sky
where the great sun stalked and shook his
  mane
and roared so brightly across the grain

it burned and shimmered like alien sands.—
Ten years old, I saw down a lane
the thunderous light on Wonderstrands.

In ages before the world ran dry,
what might the mapless not contain?
Atlantis gleamed like a dream to die,
Avalon lay under faerie reign,
Cíbola guarded a golden plain,
Tir-nan-Og was fair-locked Fand's,
sober men saw from a gull's-road wain
the thunderous light on Wonderstrands.

Such clanging countries in cloudland lie;
but men grew weary and they grew sane
and they grew grown—and so did I—
and knew Tartessus was only Spain.
No galleons call at Taprobane
(Ceylon, with English); no queenly hands
wear gold from Punt; nor sees the Dane
the thunderous light on Wonderstrands.

Ahoy, Prince Andros Horizon's-bane!
They always wait, the elven lands.
An evening planet gives again
the thunderous light on Wonderstrands.

                                        —Poul Anderson

THE INNOCENT ARRIVAL

The visiphone chimed when Peri had just gotten into her dinner gown. She peeled it off again and slipped on a casual bathrobe— a wisp of translucence which had set the president of Antarctic Enterprises, or had it been the chairman of the board, back several thousand dollars. Then she pulled a lock of lion-colored hair down over one eye, checked with a mirror, rumpled it a tiny bit more and wrapped the robe loosely on top and tight around the hips.

After all, some of the men who knew her private number were important.

She undulated to the phone and pressed its Accept. "Hello-o, there," she said automatically. "So sorry to keep you waiting, I was just taking a bath and—Oh. It's you."

Gus Doran's prawn-like eyes popped at her.

"Holy Success," he whispered in awe. "You sure the wires can carry that much voltage?"

"Well, hurry up with whatever it is," snapped Peri. "I got a date tonight."

"I'll say you do! With a Martian."

"Hm?" Peri widened her silver-blue gaze and flapped sooty lashes at him. "You must have heard wrong, Gus. He's the heir apparent of Indonesia, Inc., that's who, and if you called up to ask for a piece of him you can just blank right out again. I saw him first!"

Doran's thin sharp face grinned. "I know what I'd like a piece of," he said. "But you break that date, Peri. Put it off or something. I got this Martian for you, see?"

"So? Since when has all Mars had as much spending money as one big-time marijuana rancher? Not to mention the heir ap—"

"Sure, sure. But how much are those boys going to spend on any girl, even a high-level type like you? Listen, I need you just for tonight, see? This Martian is a whack. Strictly from gone. He is here on official business, but he is a yokel and I do mean hayseed. Like he asked me what the Christmas decorations in all the stores were! And this is the solar nexus of it, Peri, kid." Doran leaned forward as if to climb out of the screen. "He has got a hundred million dollars expense money, and they are not going to audit his accounts at home. One hundred million good green certificates, legal tender anywhere in the United Protectorates. And he has about as much backbone as a piece of steak alga. Kid, if I did

not happen to have a small nephew I would say
this will be like taking candy from a baby."

Peri's peaches-and-cream countenance began
to resemble peaches and cream left overnight
on Pluto. "Badger?" she asked.

"Sure. You and Sam Wendt handle the routine.
I will take the go-between angle, so he will think
of me as still his friend, because I have other
plans for him too. But if we can't shake a million out of him for this one night's work there is
something akilter. And your share of a million
is three hundred thirty-three—"

"Is five hundred thousand flat," said Peri. "Too
bad I just got an awful headache and can't see
Mr. Sastro tonight. Where you at, Gus?"

The gravity was not as hard to take as Peter
Matheny had expected. Three generations on
Mars might lengthen the legs and expand the
chest a trifle, but the genes had come from Earth
and the organism readjusts. What set him gasp-
ing was the air. It weighed like a ton of wool
and had apparently sopped up half the Atlantic
Ocean. Ears trained to listen through the Martian atmosphere shuddered from the racket conducted by Earth's. The passport official seemed
to bellow at him.

"Pardon me for asking this. The United Protectorates welcome all visitors to Earth, and I assure you, sir, an ordinary five-year visa provokes
no questions. But since you came on an official
courier boat of your planet, Mr. Matheny, regu-
lations force me to ask your business."

"Well . . . recruiting."

The official patted his comfortable stomach, iridescent in neolon, and chuckled patronizingly. "I am afraid, sir, you won't find many people who wish to leave. They wouldn't be able to see the Teamsters Hour on Mars, would they?"

"Oh, we don't expect immigration," said Matheny shyly. He was a fairly young man but small, with a dark-thatched snub-nosed gray-eyed head that seemed too large for his slender body. "We learned long ago no one is interested any more in giving up even second-class citizenship on Earth to live in the Republic. But we only wanted to hire . . . uh, I mean engage . . . an, an adviser. . . . We're not businessmen, we know our export trade hasn't a chance among all your corporations unless we get some—a five-year contract—?" He heard his words trailing off idiotically, and swore at himself.

"Well, good luck." The official's tone was skeptical. He stamped the passport and handed it back. "There, now, you are free to travel anywhere in the Protectorates. But I would advise you to leave the capital and get into the sticks—er-hum, I mean the provinces—I am sure there must be tolerably competent sales executives in Russia or Congolese Belgium or such regions. Frankly, sir, I do not believe you can attract anyone out of Newer York."

"Thanks," said Matheny, "but you see . . . I . . . we need . . . that is. . . . Oh, well. Thanks. Goodbye." He backed out of the office.

A dropshaft deposited him on a walkway. The crowd, a rainbow of men in pajamas and cloaks, women in Neo-Cretan dresses and goldleaf hats, swept him against the rail. For a moment, squashed to the wire, he stared a hundred feet down at a river of automobiles. *Phobos!* he thought wildly. *If the barrier gives, I'll be sliced in two by a dorsal fin before I hit the pavement!*

The August twilight wrapped him in heat and stickiness. He could see neither stars nor even moon through the city's blaze. The forest of multi-colored towers, cataracting half a mile skyward across more acreage than his eyes reached, was impressive and all that, but—he used to stroll out in the rock garden behind his cottage and smoke a pipe in company with Orion. On summer evenings, that is, when the night temperature wasn't too far below zero.

Why did they tap me for this job? he asked himself in a surge of homesickness. What the hell was the Martian Embassy here for? He, Peter Matheny, was no more than a peaceful little professor of sociodynamics at Devil's Kettle University. Of course, he had advised his government before now, in fact the Red Ānkh Society had been his idea, but still he was only at ease with his books and his chess and his mineral collection, a faculty poker party on Tenthday night and an occasional trip to Swindletown—*My God*, thought Matheny, *here I am, one solitary outlander in the greatest commercial empire the human race has even seen, and I'm supposed to find my planet a con man!*

He began walking, disconsolately at random. His lizardskin shirt and black culottes drew glances, but derisive ones: their cut was forty years out of date. He should find himself a hotel, he thought drearily, but he wasn't tired; the spaceport would pneumo his baggage to him whenever he did check in. The few Martians who had been to Earth had gone into ecstasies over the automation which put any service you could name on a twenty-four-hour basis. But it would be a long time before Mars had such machines. If ever.

The city roared at him.

He fumbled after his pipe. *Of course,* he told himself, *that's why the Embassy can't act. I may find it advisable to go outside the law. Please, sir, where can I contact the underworld?*

He wished gambling were legal on Earth. The Constitution of the Martian Republic forbade sumptuary and moral legislation; quite apart from the rambunctious individualism which that document formulated, the article was a practical necessity. Life was bleak enough on the deserts, without being denied the pleasure of trying to bottom deal some friend who was happily trying to mark the cards. Matheny would have found a few spins of roulette soothing: it was always an intellectual challenge to work out the system by which the management operated a wheel. But more, he would have been among people he understood. The frightful thing about the Earthman was the way he seemed to exist only in organized masses. A gypsy snake oil peddler, plodding his syrtosaur wagon across Martian sands just didn't have a prayer against, say, the Grant, Harding & Adams Public Relations Agency.

Matheny puffed smoke and looked around. His

feet ached from the weight on them. Where could
a man sit down? It was hard to make out any
individual sign, through all that shimmering
neon. His eye fell on one distinguished by relative austerity.

THE CHURCH OF YOUR CHOICE
Enter, Rest, and Pray

That would do. He took an upward slideramp
through several hundred feet of altitude, stepped
past an aurora curtain, and found himself in a
marble lobby next to an inspirational newsstand.

"Ah, brother, welcome," said a redhaired ush-
erette in demure black leotards. "The peace that
passeth all understanding be with you. The res-
taurant is right up those stairs."

"I . . . I'm not hungry," stammered Matheny.
"I just wanted to sit in—"

"To your left, sir."

The Martian crossed the lobby. His pipe went
out in the breeze from an animated angel. Or-
gan music sighed through an open doorway.
The series of rooms beyond was dim, Gothic,
and interminable.

"Get your chips right here, sir," said the girl
in the booth.

"Hm?" said Matheny.

She explained. He bought a few hundred-dollar
tokens, dropped a fifty-buck coin down the slot
marked CONTRIBUTIONS, and sipped the martini he got back while he strolled around studying the games. It was a good martini, probably
sold below cost. He decided that the roulette

wheels were either honest or too deep for him. He'd have to relax with a crap game instead.

He had been standing at the table for some time before the rest of the congregation really noticed him. Then it was with awe. The first few passes he had made were unsuccessful, Earth gravity threw him off, but when he got the rhythm of it he tossed a row of sevens. It was a customary form of challenge on Mars. Here, though, they simply pushed chips toward him. He missed a throw as anyone would at home: simple courtesy. The next time around he threw for a seven just to get the feel. He got a seven. The dice had not been substituted on him.

"I say," he exclaimed. He looked up into eyes and eyes, all around the green table. "I'm sorry. I guess I don't know your rules."

"You did all right, brother," said a middle-aged lady with an obviously surgical nonbodice.

"But—I mean . . . when do we start actually *playing?* What happened to the cocked dice?"

"Sir!" The lady drew herself up and jutted an indignant prow at him. "This is a church!"

"Oh . . . I see . . . excuse me, I, I, I—" Matheny backed out of the crowd, shuddering. He looked around for some place to hide his burning ears.

"You forgot your chips, pal," said a voice.

"Oh. Thanks. Thanks ever so much. I, I, that is—" Matheny cursed his knotting tongue. *Damn it, just because they're so much more sophisticated than I, do I have to talk like a leaky boiler?*

The helpful Earthman was not tall, he was dark and chiselfaced and sleekly pomaded, dapper in blue pajamas with a red zig-zag, a sleighbell cloak and curly-toed slippers. "You're from Mars, aren't you?" he asked in the friendliest tone Matheny had yet heard.

"Yes. Yes, I am. M-my name's Peter Matheny, I, I—" He stuck out his hand to shake and chips rolled over the floor. "Damn! Oh, excuse me, I forgot this was a church. Never mind them! No, please, I just want to g-g-get the hell out of here."

"Good idea. How about a drink? I know a bar downshaft."

Matheny sighed. "A drink I need the very most."

"My name's Doran. Gus Doran. Call me Gus." They walked back to the deaconette's booth and Matheny cashed what remained of his winnings.

"I don't want to, I mean, if you're busy tonight, Mr. Doran—"

"Nah. I am not doing one thing in particular. Besides, I have never met a Martian. I am very interested."

"There aren't many of us on Earth," agreed Matheny. "Just a small embassy staff and an occasional like me."

"I should think you would do a lot of traveling here. The old mother planet and so on."

"We can't afford it," said Matheny. "What with gravitation and distance, such voyages are much too expensive for us to make them for pleasure. Not to mention our dollar shortage." As they entered the shaft, he added wistfully: "You Earth people have that kind of money, at least in your more prosperous brackets. Why don't you send a few tourists to us?"

"I always wanted to," said Doran. "I would like to see the, what they call, City of Time, and so on. As a matter of fact, I have given my girl one of those Old Martian rings last Ike's Birthday, and she was just gazoo about it. A jewel dug out of the City of Time, like, made a million years ago by a, uh, extinct race ... I tell you, she *appreciated* me for it!" He winked and nudged.

"Oh," said Matheny. He felt a certain guilt. Doran was too pleasant a little man to deserve— "Of course," he said ritually, "I agree with all the archeologists it's a crime to sell such scientifically priceless artifacts, but what can we do? We must live, and the tourist trade is almost nonexistent."

"Trouble with it is, I hear Mars is not so comfortable," said Doran. "I mean, do not get me wrong, I don't want to insult you or anything, but people come back saying you have given the planet just barely enough air to keep a man alive. And it gets so cold that soon even the dimmest lady tourist gets the idea of that Brass Monkey Memorial you have erected. And there are no cities, just little towns and villages and ranches out in the bush—I mean, you are being pioneers and making a new nation and all that, but people paying half a megabuck for their ticket expect some comfort and, uh, you know."

"I do know," said Matheny. "But we're poor! We're a handful of people trying to make a world of dust and sand and scrub thorn into fields and woods and seas. We can't do it without substantial help from Earth, equipment and supplies— which can only be paid for in Earth dollars—and we can't export enough to Earth to earn those dollars.''

By that time they were entering the Paul Bunyan Knotty Pine Bar & Grill, on the 73rd level. Matheny's jaw clanked down. "Whassa matter?" asked Doran. "Ain't you ever seen a ecdysiastic technician before?"

"Uh, yes, but . . . well . . . not in a 3-D image under ten magnifications." Matheny followed Doran past a sign announcing that this show was for purely artistic purposes, into a booth. There a soundproof curtain reduced the noise level enough so they could talk in normal voices.

"What'll you have?" asked Doran. "It's on me."

"Oh, I couldn't let you. I mean—"

"Nonsense. Welcome to Earth! Care for a Thyle and vermouth?"

Matheny shuddered. "Good Lord, no!"

"Huh? But they make Thyle right on Mars, don't they?"

"Yes. And it all goes to Earth and sells at 2000 dollars a fifth. But you don't think we'd *drink* it, do you? I mean, well, I imagine it doesn't absolutely ruin vermouth. But we don't see those Earthside commercials about how sophisticated people like it so much."

"Well, I'll be a socialist creeper!" Doran's face split in a grin. "You know, all my life I've hated the stuff and never dared admit it?" He raised a hand. "Don't worry, I won't blabbo. But I am wondering, if you control the Thyle industry, and sell all those relics at fancy prices . . . why do you call yourselves poor?"

"Because we are," said Matheny. "By the time the shipping costs have been paid on a bottle, and the Earth wholesaler and jobber and sales engineer and so on, down to the retailer, have taken their percentage, and the advertising agency has been paid, and about fifty separate Earth taxes ... there's very little profit going back to the distillery on Mars. The same principle is what's strangling us on everything. Old Martian artifacts aren't really rare, for instance, but freight charges and the middlemen here put them out of the mass market."

"Have you not got some other businesses?"

"Well, we do sell a lot of color slides, postcards, baggage labels, and so on to people who like to act cosmopolitan; and I understand our travel posters are quite popular as wall decoration. But all that has to be printed on Earth, and the printer and distributor keep most of the money. We've sold some books and show tapes, of course, but only one has been really successful—*I Was a Slave Girl on Mars*. Our most prominent novelist was co-opted to ghostwrite that one. Again, though, your income taxes took most of the money; authors never have been protected the way a businessman is. We do make a high percentage of profit on those little certificates you see around—you know, the title deeds to one square inch of Mars—but expressed absolutely, in dollars, it doesn't amount to much when we start shopping for bulldozers and thermo-nuclear power plants."

"How about postage stamps?" inquired Doran. "Philately is a big business, I have heard."

"It was our mainstay," admitted Matheny, "but it's been overworked. Martian stamps are a drug on the market. What we'd like to operate is a sweepstakes, but the antigambling laws on Earth forbid that."

Doran whistled. "I got to give you people credit for enterprise, anyway!" He fingered his mustache. "Uh, pardon me, but have you tried to, well, attract capital from Earth?"

"Of course," said Matheny bitterly. "We offer the most liberal concessions in the Solar System. Any little mining company or transport firm or . . . or anybody . . . who wanted to come and actually invest a few dollars in Mars—why, we'd probably give him the President's daughter as security. No, the Minister of Ecology has a better-looking one. But who's interested? Mars is forty million miles away at closest. We haven't a thing that Earth hasn't got more of. We're only the descendants of a few scientists, a few political malcontents, oddballs who happen to prefer el-bow room and a bill of liberties to the incorpo-rated state—what could General Nucleonics hope to get from Mars?"

"I see. Well, what are you having to drink?"

"Beer," said Matheny without hesitation.

"Huh? Look, pal, this is on me."

"The only beer on Mars comes forty million miles, with interplanetary freight charges tacked on," said Matheny. "Tuborg!"

Doran shrugged, dialed the dispenser and fed it coins.

"This is a real interesting talk, Pete," he said.

"You are being very frank with me. I like a man that is frank."

Matheny shrugged. "I haven't told you anything that isn't known to every economist."

Of course I haven't. I've not so much as mentioned the Red Ānkh, for instance. But in principle, I have told him the truth, told him of our need; for even the secret operations do not yield us enough.

The beer arrived. Matheny engulfed himself in it. Doran sipped at a whiskey sour and unobtrusively set a fresh brew in front of the Martian.

"Ahhh!" said Matheny. "Bless you, my friend."

"A pleasure."

"But now you must let me buy you one."

"That is not necessary. After all," said Doran with great tact, "with the situation as you have been describing—"

"Oh, we're not that poor! My expense allowance assumes I will entertain quite a bit."

Doran's brows lifted a few minutes of arc. "You're here on business, then?"

"Yes. I told you we haven't any tourists. I was sent to hire a business manager for the Martian export trade."

"What's wrong with your own people? I mean, Pete, it is not your fault there are so many rackets . . . uh, taxes . . . and middlemen and agencies and et cetera. That is just the way Earth is set up these days."

"Exactly." Matheny's finger stabbed in the general direction of Doran's pajama top. "And who set it up that way? Earthmen. We Martians are babes in the bush. What chance do we have to earn dollars on the scale we need them, in competition with corporations which could buy and sell our whole planet before breakfast? Why, we couldn't afford three seconds of commercial time on a Lullaby Pillow 'cast. What we need, what we have to hire, is an executive who knows Earth, who's an Earthman himself. Let him tell us what will appeal to your people, and how to dodge the tax bite and . . . and, well, you see how it goes, that sort of, uh, thing." Matheny felt his eloquence running down and grabbed for the second bottle of beer.

"But where do I start?" he asked plaintively, for his loneliness smote him anew. "I'm just a college professor at home. How would I even get to see—"

"It might be arranged," said Doran in a thoughtful tone. "It just might. How much could you pay this fellow?"

"A hundred megabucks a year, if he'll sign a five-year contract. That's Earth years, mind you."

"I'm sorry to tell you this, Pete," said Doran, "but while that is not bad money, it is not what a high-powered sales scientist gets in Newer York. Plus his retirement benefits, which he would lose if he quit where he is now at. And I am sure he would not want to settle on Mars permanently."

"I could offer a certain amount of, uh, well, lagniappe," said Matheny. "That is, well, I can draw up to a hundred megabucks myself for, uh, expenses and, well . . . let me buy you a drink!"

Doran's black eyes frogged at him. "You might at that," said the Earthman very softly. "Yes, you might at that."

Matheny found himself warming. Gus Doran was a thentic bobber. A hell of a swell chap. He explained modestly that he was a free lance business consultant and it was barely possible he could arrange some contacts . . . no, no, no commission, all done in the interest of interplanetary friendship . . . well, anyhow, let's not talk business now. If you have got to stick to beer, Pete, make it a chaser to akvavit. What is akvavit? Well, I will just take and show you.

A hell of a good bloke. He knew some very funny stories, too, and he laughed at Matheny's, though they were probably too rustic for a big city taste like his.

"What I really want," said Matheny, "what I really want, I mean, what Mars really needs, get me?—is a confidence man."

"A what?"

"The best and slickest one on Earth, to operate a world-size con game for us and make us some *real* money."

"Con man—Oh. A slipstring."

"A con by any other name," said Matheny, pouring down an akvavit.

"Hm." Doran squinted through cigaret smoke. "You are interesting me strangely, my friend. Say on."

"No." Matheny realized his head was a bit smoky. The walls of the booth seemed odd, somehow. They were just leatheroid walls, but they had an odd quality.

"No, sorry, Gus," he said. "I spoke too much."

"Okay. Forget it. I do not like a man that

pries. But look, let's bomb out of here, how about it? Go have a little fun."

"By all means." Matheny disposed of his last beer. "I could use some gaiety."

"You have come to the right town, then. But let us get you a hotel room first and some more up to date clothes."

"*Allez*," said Matheny. "If I don't mean *allons*, or maybe *alors*."

The drop down to cabramp level and the short ride afterward sobered him; the room rate at the Jupiter-Astoria sobered him still more. *Oh, well*, he thought, *if I succeed in this job no one at home will quibble*. And the chamber to which he and Doran were shown was spectacular enough, with a pneumo direct to the bar and a full-wall transparency to show the vertical incandescence of the towers.

"Whoof!" Matheny sat down. The chair slithered sensuously about his contours. He jumped. "What the dusty hell—Oh." He tried to grin, but his face burned. "I see."

"That is a sexy type of furniture, all right," agreed Doran. He lowered himself into another chair, cocked his feet on the 3-D, and waved a cigarette. "Which speaking of, what say we get some girls? It is not too late to catch them at home, a date here will usually start around 2100 hours earliest."

"What?"

"You know. Dames. Like a certain blonde warhead with twin radar globes and swivel mounting, and she just loves exotics. Such as you."

"Me?" Matheny heard his voice climb to a

schoolboy squeak. "Me? Exotic? Why, I'm just a little college professor, I, g-g-g, that is—" His tongue got stuck on his palate. He pulled it loose and moistened uncertain lips.

"You are from Mars. Okay? So you fought bushcats barehanded in an abandoned canal."

"What's a bushcat? And we don't have canals. The evaporation rate—"

"Look, Pete," said Doran patiently. "She don't have to know that, does she?"

"Well, well, no. I guess not. No."

"Let's order you some clothes on the pneumo," said Doran. "I recommend you buy from Schwartz-herz, everybody knows he is expensive."

While Matheny jittered about, shaving and showering and struggling with his new raiment, Doran kept him supplied with akvavit and beer. "You said one thing, Pete," he remarked. "About needing a slipstring. A con man, you would call it."

"Forget that. Please. I spoke out of turn."

"Well, you see, maybe a man like that is just what Mars does need. And maybe I have got a few contacts."

"What?" Matheny gaped out of the bathroom.

Doan cupped his hands around a fresh cigarette, not looking at him. "I am not that man," he said frankly. "But in my line I get a lot of contacts, and not all of them go topside. See what I mean? Like if, say, you wanted some-body terminated, and could pay for it, I could not do it. I would not want to know anything about it. But I could tell you a phone number."

He shrugged and gave the Martian a sidelong

glance. "Sure, you may not be interested. But if you are, well, Pete, I was not born yesterday. I got tolerance. Like the Good Book says, if you want to get ahead, you have got to think positively. And your mission is pretty important."

Matheny hesitated. If only he hadn't taken that last shot—! It made him want to say yes, immediately, without reservations. And therefore maybe he became over-cautious.

They had instructed him on Mars to take chances if he must.

"I could tell you a thing or two which might give you a better idea," he said slowly. "But it would have to be under security."

"Okay by me. Room service can send us up an oath right now."

"What? But—but—" Matheny hung onto himself and tried to believe that he had landed on Earth less than six hours ago.

In the end he did call room service and the machine was trundled in. Doran swallowed the pill and donned the conditioner helmet without an instant's hesitation. "I shall never reveal to any person unauthorized by yourself whatever you may tell me under security, now or at any other time," he recited. Then, cheerfully: "And that formula, Pete, happens to be the honest-to-zebra truth."

"I know." Matheny stared embarrassed at the carpet. "I'm sorry to . . . to . . . I mean, of course I trust you, but—"

"Forget it. I take a hundred security oaths a year, in my line of work. Maybe I can help you. I like you, Pete, damn if I don't. And of course I might stand to get an agent's cut, if I arrange— Go ahead, boy, go ahead." Doran crossed his legs and leaned back.

"Oh, it's simple enough," said Matheny. "It's only that we already are operating con games."

"On Mars, you mean?"

"Yes. There never were any Old Martians. We erected the ruins fifty years ago for the Billingsworth Expedition to find. We've been manufacturing relics ever since."

"Huh? Well, why, but—"

"In this case it helps to be at the far end of an interplanetary haul," said Matheny. "Not many Terrestrial archeologists get to Mars, and they depend on our people to— Well, anyhow—"

"I will be clopped! Good for you!" Doran blew up in laughter. "That is one thing I would never spill, even without security. I told you about my girl friend, didn't I?"

"Oh, yes, the Little Girl," said Matheny apologetically. "She was another official project."

"Who?"

"Remember Junie O'Brien? The little golden-haired girl on Mars, a mathematical prodigy, but dying of an incurable disease? She collected Earth coins."

"Oh, that. Sure, I remember—Hey! You didn't!"

"Yes. We made about a billion dollars on that one."

"I will be double damned. You know, Pete, I sent her a hundred buck piece myself. . . . Say, how is Junie O'Brien?"

"Oh, fine. Under a different name, she's now our finance minister." Matheny stared out the wall, his hands twisting nervously behind his back. "There were no lies involved. She really does have a fatal disease. So do you and I. Every day we grow older."

"Uh!" exclaimed Doran.

"And then the Red Ānkh Society. You must have seen or heard their ads . . . let me think . . . 'What mysterious knowledge did the Old Martians possess? What was the secret wisdom of the Ancients? Now the incredibly powerful semantics of the Red Ānkh (not a religious organization) is available to a select few—' "

"Oh, those. Sure. But aren't they out in California?"

"Just a front," said Matheny. "Actually, that's our largest dollar-earning enterprise." He would have liked to say it was his suggestion originally, but that would have been too presumptuous. He was talking to an Earthman, who had heard everything already.

Doran whistled.

"That's about all, so far," confessed Matheny. "Perhaps a con is our only hope. I've been wondering, maybe we could organize a Martian bucket shop, handling Martian securities, but— Well, I don't know."

"I think—" Doran removed the helmet and stood up.

"Yes?" Matheny faced around, shivering with his own tension.

"I may be able to find the man you want," said Doran. "I just may. It will take a few days and might get a little expensive."

"You mean ... Mr. Doran—Gus—you could actually—"

"I cannot promise anything yet except that I will try. Now you finish dressing. I will be down in the bar. And I will call up this girl I know. We deserve a celebration!"

Peri was tall. Peri was slim. Peri smoldered when she walked and exploded when she stretched. Her apartment was ivory and ebony, her sea-green dress was poured on, and the Neo-Cretan mode had obviously been engineered to her personal specifications.

She waved twelve inches of jade cigaret holder, lifted her glass, and murmured throatily: "To you, Pete. To Mars."

"I, I, I," stammered Matheny. He raised his own glass. It slopped over. "Oh, damn! I mean ... gosh, I'm so sorry, I—"

"No harm done. You aren't used to our gravity yet," Peri extended a flawless leg out of her slit skirt and turned it about on the couch, presumably in search of a more comfortable position. "And it must seem terribly cramped here on Earth, Pete," she continued, "after roaming the desert, hunting, sleeping under the twin moons. Two moons! Why, what girl could resist that?"

"Uh, well, as a matter of fact, the moons are barely visible," floundered Matheny.

Peri pouted, dimpling her cheeks. "Must you spoil my dreams?" she said. "When I think of Mars, the frontier, where men are still men, why, my breast swells with emotion."

"Uh, yes." Matheny gulped. "Swell. Yes."

She leaned closer to his chair. "Now that I've got you, don't think you'll get away," she smiled. "A live Martian, trapped!"

Doran looked at his watch. "Well," he said, "I have got to get up tomorrow, so I had better run along now."

"Ta-ta," said Peri. Matheny rose. She pulled him down beside her. "Oh, no, you don't, Mars lad. I'm not through with you yet!"

"But, but, but," said Matheny.

Doran chuckled. "I'll meet you on the Terrace at fourteen hundred hours tomorrow," he said. "Have fun, Pete."

The door closed on him.

Peri slithered toward her guest. He felt a nudge and looked down. She had not actually touched him with her hands. "Gus is a good squiff," she said, "but I wondered if he'd ever go."

"Why, why . . . what do you mean?" croaked Matheny.

"Haven't you guessed?" she whispered.

She kissed him. It was rather like being caught in a nuclear turbine, with soft blades.

Matheny, said Matheny, *you represent your planet*.

Matheny, said Matheny, *shut up*.

Time passed.

"Have another drink," said Peri, "while I slip into something more comfortable."

Her idea of comfort was modest in one sense of the word: a nightdress or something, like a breath of smoke, and a seat on Matheny's lap.

"If you kiss me like that just once more," she breathed, "I'll forget I'm a nice girl."

Matheny kissed her like that.

The door crashed open. A large man stood there, breathing heavily. *"What are you doing with my wife?"* he bawled.

"Sam!" screamed Peri. "I thought you were in Australia!"

"—and he said he might settle out of court," finished Matheny. He stared in a numb fashion at his beer. "He'll come to my hotel room this afternoon. What am I going to do?"

"It is a great shame," said Doran. "I never thought . . . you know, he told everybody he would be gone on business for weeks yet— Pete, I am more sorry than I can express."

"If he thinks I'll pay his miserable blackmail," bristled Matheny, "he can take his head and stick—"

Doran shook his own. "I am sorry, Pete, but I would pay if I was you. He does have a case. It is too bad he just happened to be carrying that loaded camera, but he is a photographer and now, well, our laws on Earth are pretty strict about unlicensed corespondents. You could be very heavily fined as well as deported, plus all the civil damage claims and the publicity. It would ruin your mission and even make trouble for the next man Mars sent."

"But," stuttered Matheny, "b-but it's a badger game!"

"Look," said Doran. He leaned over the table and gripped the Martian's shoulder. "I am your friend, see? I feel real bad this happened. In a way it is my fault and I want to help you. So let me go talk to Sam Wendt. I will cool him down if I can. I will talk down his figure. It will still cost you, Pete, but fout, you can pad your expense account, can't you? So we will both come see you today. That way there will be two people on your side, you and me, and Sam will not throw his weight around so much. You pay up in cash and it will be the end of the affair. I will see to that, pal!"

Matheny stared at the small dapper man. His aloneness came to him like a blow in the stomach. *Et tu, Brute*, he thought.

He bit his lip. "Thanks, Gus," he said. "You are a real friend."

Sam blocked the doorway with his shoulders as he entered the room. Doran followed like a diminutive tug pushing a very large liner. They closed the door. Matheny stood up, avoiding Sam's glare.

"Okay, louse," harshed Sam. "You got a better pal here than you deserve, but he ain't managed to talk me into settling for nothing."

"Let me get this ... I mean ... well," said Matheny. "Look, sir, you claim that I, I mean that your wife and I were, uh, well, we weren't. Not really. I was only visiting her and—"

"Stow it, stow it." Sam towered over the Martian. "Shoot it to the moon. You had your fun. It'll cost you. One million dollars."

"One mil—But—but—Gus," wailed Matheny, "this is out of all reason! I thought you said—"

Doran shrugged. "I am sorry, Pete. I could not get him any farther down. He started asking fifty. You better pay him."

"No!" Matheny scuttled behind a chair. "No, look here! I, Peter Matheny of the Martian Republic, declare you are blackmailing me!"

"I'm asking compensation for damages," growled Sam. "Hand it over or I'll go talk to a lawyer. That ain't blackmail. You got your choice, don't you?"

Matheny wilted. "Yes," he shuddered.

"A megabuck isn't so bad, Pete," soothed Doran. "I personally, will see that you earn it back in—"

"Oh, never mind." Tears stood in Matheny's eyes. "You win." He took out his checkbook.

"None of that," rapped Sam. "Cash. Now."

"But you claimed this was a legitimate—"

"You heard me."

"Well . . . could I have a receipt?" begged Matheny.

Sam grinned.

"I just thought I'd ask," said Matheny.

He opened a drawer and counted out one hundred ten-kilo-buck bills. "There! And, and, and I hope you choke on it!"

Sam stuffed the money in a pocket and lumbered out.

Doran lingered. "Look here, Pete," he said, "I will make this up to you. Honest. All you have got to do is trust me."

"Sure." Matheny slumped on the bed. "Not your fault. Let me alone for a while, will you?"

"Look, I will come back in a few hours and

buy you the best dinner in all the Protectorates and—"

"Sure," said Matheny. "Sure."

Doran left, closing the door with great gentleness.

He returned at 1730, entered, and stopped dead. The floor space was half taken up by a screen and a film projector. "What happened, Pete?" he asked uncertainly.

Matheny smiled. "I took some tourist movies," he said. "Self-developing soundtrack film. Sit down, and I'll show you."

"Well, thanks, but I am not so much for home movies."

"It won't take long. Please."

Doran shrugged, found a chair, and took out a cigarette. "You seem pretty well cheered up now," he remarked. "That is a spirit I like to see. You have got to have faith."

"I'm thinking of a sideline business in live photography," said the Martian. "Get back my losses of today, you know."

"Well, now, Pete, I like your spirit, like I say. But if you are really interested in making some of that old baroom, and I think you are, then listen—"

"I'll sell prints to people for home viewing," went on Matheny. "I'd like your opinion of this first effort." He dimmed the transparency and started the projector. The screen sprang into colored motion. Sam Wendt blocked the doorway with his shoulders.

"Who knows, I might even sell you one of the several prints I made today," said Matheny.

. . . "Okay, louse," said Sam. . . .

"Life is hard on Mars," commented Matheny in an idle tone, "and we're an individualistic culture. The result is pretty fierce competition, though on a person-to-person rather than organizational basis. All friendly enough, but—Oh, by the way, how do you like our Martian camera technology? I wore this one inside my buttonhole."

Doran in the screen shrugged and said: "I am sorry, Pete." Doran in the chair stubbed out his cigarette, very carefully, and asked, "How much do you want for that film?"

"Would a megabuck be a fair price?" inquired Matheny.

"Uh . . . huh."

"Of course, I am hoping Sam will want a copy too."

Doran swallowed. "Yeah. Yes, I think I can talk him into it."

"Good." Matheny stopped the projector. He sat down on the edge of the table, swinging one leg, and lit his pipe. Its bowl glowed in the dimness like the eye of a small demon. "By the way," he said irrelevantly, "if you check newscast tapes you'll find I was runner-up in last year's all-Martian pistol contest. We shoot from the hip."

"I see." Doran wet his lips. "Uh, no hard feelings. No, none at all. But say, in case you are, well, you know, looking for a slipstring, what I came here for was to tell you I have located the very guy you want. Only he is in jail right now, see, and it will cost—"

"Oh, no!" groaned Matheny. "Not the Syrtis Prospector! Kids are taught that one in kindergarten."

Doran bowed his head. "We call it the Spanish Prisoner here," he said. He got up. "I will send the price of those films around in the morning."

"You'll call your bank and have the cash pneumoed here tonight," said Matheny. "Also Sam's share. I daresay he can pay you back."

"No harm in trying, was there?" asked Doran humbly.

"None at all," said Matheny. He chuckled. "In fact, I'm grateful to you. You helped me solve my major problem."

"What?"

"I'll have to investigate further, but I'm sure my hunch will be confirmed. You see, we Martians have stood in awe of Earthmen. And since for a long time there's been very little contact between the two planets except the purely official, impersonal sort, there's been nothing to disabuse us. It's certainly true that our organizations can't compete with yours, because your whole society is based on organizations.—But now, by the same token, I wonder if your individuals can match ours. Ever hear of the Third Moon? No? the whipsaw play? The aqueduct squeeze? Good Lord, can't you even load a derrel set?" Matheny licked his chops. "So there's our Martian export to Earth. Martian con men. I tell you this under security, of course—not that anyone would believe you, till our boys walk home with the shirt off the Terrestrial back."

He waved an imperious pipestem. "Hurry up and pay me, please. I've a date tonight with Peri. I just called her up and explained the situation, and she really does seem to like Martians."

—Poul and Karen Anderson

SIX HAIKU

1

The white vapor trail
  Scrawls slowly on the sky
    Without any squeak.

2

Gilt and painted clouds
  Float back through the shining air,
    What, are there stars, too?

3

In the heavy world's
  Shadow, I watch the sputnik
    Coasting in sunlight.

4

Those crisp cucumbers
  Not yet planted in Syrtis—
    How I desire one!

5

In the fantastic
  Seas of Venus, who would dare
    To imagine gulls?

6

When Proxima sets
  What constellation do they
  Dream around our sun?

—KAREN ANDERSON

HAIKU FOR MARS

I

From this neighbor hill
   The noonday of Mars outshines
     The windows of home.

II

For one who goes forth,
   For one who sees the tall ship
     Depart: two wonders.

III

On Syrtis, we lay
   Foundations for the topless
     Towers of Helium.

IV

I watch the dust scud
   Past my faceplate, and wonder:
     What does it smell like?

—Karen Anderson

THINK OF A MAN

Think of a man—and think he's much like you—
   Who cups like gems in memory's hand the
   stars
And maybe says: "This one that blazes blue
   Shone down—near crisped me!—on the Canis
   wars.
   I was decorated: medal and three scars.
Next came this yellow, Procyon; by its light
   I spent some gritty months in desert cars,
Drank up my pay and hoped there'd be no fight.

"And then to Pollux; not so bright, but warm;
   Just like the girl I met there—comfort, though,
Can get damned dull. My dress whites were the
   charm
   That kept her, and I shed them; shed her so.
   A merchant ticket hauled me, come and go,
A dozen times round Castor and Capella.
   Castor's this green one: dazzled on the snow
That slipped me up and cracked my fool patella.

"I thought I liked it dirtside; learned to gamble
   The one sure way to win—got paid to deal.
And that got dull. I took a little amble
   To this one, arc-blue Regulus, to feel
   Once more the thrum and urge of driven steel.
Sudden I hated day-star never changing
   And suns at night held all to one round wheel.
I knew for me there'd be no life but ranging."

Think then of such a man, who gems his thought
　　With Mizar's emerald, Vega's diamond gleam,
Arcturus' topaz: wealth he's fairly bought
　　With nothing less than heartblood. Let him
　　seem
　　Grown old, with darting eyes whose corners
　　teem
Wrinkles to laugh like dawn or weep like dew:
　　Hell-tested, Heaven blest: he lives his dream.
　　Think such a man. And think he might be you.

　　　　　　　　　　　　　—KAREN ANDERSON

DEAD PHONE

That was an evil autumn, when the powers bared their teeth across an island in the Spanish Main and it seemed the world might burn. Afterward Americans looked at each other with a kind of wonder, and for a while they walked more straight. But whatever victory they had gained was soon taken away from them.

As if to warn, a fortnight earlier the weather ran amok. On the Pacific coast, gale force winds flung sea against land, day and night without end, and rainfall in northern California redressed the balance of a three-year drought in less than a week. At the climax of it, the hills around San Francisco Bay started to come down in mudslides that took houses and human bodies along, and the streets of some towns were turned into rivers.

Trygve Yamamura sat up late. His wife had taken the children to visit her cousin in the

Mother Lode country over the Columbus Day weekend. His work kept him behind; so now he prowled the big hollow house on the Berkeley steeps, smoked one pipe after another, listened to the wind and the rain lashing his roof and to the radio whose reports grew ever more sinister, and could not sleep.

Oh, yes, he told himself often and often, he was being foolish. They had undoubtedly arrived without trouble and were now snug at rest. In any event, he could do nothing to help, he was only exhausting himself, in violation of his entire philosophy. Tomorrow morning the phone line that had snapped, somewhere in those uplands, would be repaired, and he would hear their voices. But meanwhile his windowpanes were holes of blackness, and he started when a broken tree branch crashed against the wall.

He sought his basement gym and tried to exercise himself into calm. That didn't work either, simply added a different kind of weariness. He was worn down, he knew, badly in need of a vacation, with no immediate prospect of one. His agency had too many investigations going for him to leave the staff unsupervised.

He was also on edge because through various connections he knew more about the Cuban situation than had yet gotten into the papers. A nuclear showdown was beginning to look all too probable. Yamamura was not a pacifist, even when it came to that kind of war; but no sane man, most especially no man with wife and children, could coolly face abomination.

Toward midnight he surrendered. The Zen

subject

PS
3551

techniques had failed, or he had. His eyes felt
hot and his brain gritty. He stripped, stood long
under the shower, and at last, with a grimace,
swallowed a sleeping pill.

The drug took quick hold of his unaccustomed
body, but nonetheless he tossed about half awake
and half in nightmare. It gibbered through his
head, he stumbled among terrors and guilts, the
sun had gone black while horrible stars rained
down upon him. When the phone beside his bed
rang he struck out with his fists and gasped.

Brring! the bell shouted across a light-year of
wind and voices, *brring,* come to me, you must
you must before that happens which has no
name, *brring, brring,* you are damned to come
and *brring* me her *brring brring brrRING!*

He struggled to wake. Night strangled him.
He could not speak or see, so great was his need
of air. The receiver made lips against his ear
and kissed him obscenely while the dark giggled.
Through whirl and seethe he heard a click, then
a whistle that went on forever, and he had a
moment to think that the noise was not like any
in this world, it was as if he had a fever or as if
nothing was at the other end of the line except
the huntsman wind. His skull resounded with
the querning of the planets. Yet when the voice
came it was clear, steady, a little slow and very
sad—but how remote, how monstrously far away.

"Come to me. It's so dark here."

Yamamura lay stiff in his own darkness.

"I don't understand," said the voice. "I thought
. . . afterward I would know everything, or else

nothing. But instead I don't understand. Oh, God, but it's lonely!"

For a space only the humming and the chill whistle were heard. Then: "Why did I call you, Trygve Yamamura? For help? What help is there now? You don't even know that we don't understand afterward. Were those pigs that I heard grunting in the forest, and did she come behind them in a black cloak? I'm all alone."

And presently: "Something must be left. I read somewhere once that you don't die in a piece. The last and lowest cells work on for hours. I guess that's true. Because you're still real, Trygve Yamamura." Anther pause, as if for the thoughtful shaking of a weary head. "Yes, that must be why I called. What became of me, no, that's of no account any more. But the others. They won't stay real for very long. I had to call while they are, so you can help them. Come."

"Cardynge," Yamamura mumbled.

"No," said the voice. "Goodbye."

The instrument clicked off. Briefly the thin screaming continued along the wires, and then it too died, and nothing remained but the weight in Yamamura's hand.

He became conscious of the storm that dashed against the windows, fumbled around and snapped the lamp switch. The bedroom sprang into existence: warm yellow glow on the walls, mattress springy beneath him and covers tangled above, the bureau with the children's pictures on top. The clock said 1:35. He stared at the receiver before laying it back in its cradle.

"Whoof," he said aloud.

Had he dreamed that call? No, he couldn't have. As full awareness flowed into him, every nerve cried alarm. His lanky, thick-chested frame left the bed in one movement. Yanking the directory from its shelf below the stand, he searched for an address. Yes, here. He took the phone again and dialed.

"Berkeley police," said a tone he recognized.

"Joe? This is Trig Yamamura. I think I've got some trouble to report. Client of mine just rang me up. Damndest thing I ever heard, made no sense whatsoever, but he seems to be in a bad way and the whole thing suggests—" Yamamura stopped.

"Yes, what?" said the desk officer.

Yamamura pinched his lips together before he said, "I don't know. But you'd better send a car around to have a look."

"Trig, do *you* feel right? Don't you know what's happening outdoors? We may get a disaster call any minute, if a landslide starts, and we've got our hands full as is with emergencies."

"You mean this is too vague?" Yamamura noticed the tension that knotted his muscles. One by one he forced them to relax. "Okay, I see your point," he said. "But you know I don't blow the whistle for nothing, either. Dispatch a car as soon as possible, if you don't hear anything else from me. Meanwhile I'll get over there myself. The place isn't far from here."

"M-m-m . . . well, fair enough, seeing it's you. Who is the guy and where does he live?"

"Aaron Cardynge." Yamamura spelled the name and gave the address he had checked.

"Oh, yeah, I've heard of him. Medium-big importer, isn't he? I guess he wouldn't rouse you without some reason. Go ahead, then, and we'll alert the nearest car to stop by when it can."

"Thanks." Yamamura had started to skin out of his pajamas before he hung up.

He was back into his clothes, with a sweater above, very nearly as fast, and pulled on his raincoat while he kicked the garage door open. The wind screeched at him. When he backed the Volkswagen out, it trembled with that violence. Rain roared on its metal and flooded down the windshield; his headlights and the rear lamps were quickly gulped down by night. Through everything he could hear how water cascaded along the narrow, twisting hill streets and sheeted under his wheels. The brake drums must be soaked, he thought, and groped his way in second gear.

But the storm was something real to fight, that cleansed him of vague horrors. As he drove, with every animal skill at his command, he found himself thinking in a nearly detached fashion.

Why should Cardynge call me? I only met him once. And not about anything dangerous. Was it?

"I'm sorry, Mr. Cardynge," Yamamura said. "This agency doesn't handle divorce work."

The man across the desk shifted in his chair and took out a cigaret case. He was large-boned, portly, well-dressed, with gray hair brushed back

above a rugged face. "I'm not here about that."
He spoke not quite steadily and had some diffi-
culty keeping his eyes on the detective's.

"Oh? I beg your pardon. But you told me—"

"Background. I . . . I'd tell a doctor as much
as I could, too. So he'd have a better chance of
helping me. Smoke?"

"No, thanks. I'm strictly a pipe man." More
to put Cardynge at his ease than because he
wanted one, Yamamura took a briar off the rack
and charged it. "I don't know if we can help.
Just what is the problem?"

"To find my son, I said. But you should know
why he left and why it's urgent to locate him."
Cardynge lit his cigarette and consumed it in quick,
nervous puffs. "I don't like exposing my troubles.
Believe me. Always made my own way before."

Yamamura leaned back, crossed his long legs,
and regarded the other through a blue cloud.
"I've heard worse than anything you're likely to
have on your mind," he said. "Take your time."

Cardynge's troubled gaze sought the flat half-
Oriental countenance before him. "I guess the
matter isn't too dreadful at that," he said.
"Maybe not even as sordid as it looks from the
inside. And it's nearing an end now. But I've got
to find Bayard, my boy, soon.

"He's my son by my first marriage. My wife
died two years ago. I married Lisette a year
later. Indecent haste? I don't know. I'd been so
happy before. Hadn't realized how happy, till
Maria was gone and I was rattling around alone
in the house. Bayard was at the University most
of the time, you see. This would be his junior

year. He had an apartment of his own. We'd wanted him to, the extra cost was nothing to us and he should have that taste of freedom, don't you think? Afterward . . . he'd have come back to stay with me if I asked. He offered to. But, oh, call it kindness to him, or a desire to carry on what Maria and I had begun, or false pride—I said no, that wasn't necessary, I could get along fine. And I did, physically. Had a housekeeper by day but cooked my own dinner, for something to do. I'm not a bad amateur cook."

Cardynge brought himself up short, stubbed out his cigaret, and lit another. "Not relevant," he said roughly, "except maybe to show why I made my mistake. A person gets lonesome eating by himself.

"Bayard's a good boy. He did what he could for me. Mainly that amounted to visiting me pretty often. More and more, he'd bring friends from school along. I enjoyed having young people around. Maria and I had always hoped for several children.

"Lisette got included in one of those parties. She was older than the rest, twenty-five, taking a few graduate courses. Lovely creature, witty, well read, captivating manners. I . . . I asked Bayard to be sure and invite her for next time. Then I started taking her out myself. Whirlwind courtship, I suppose. I'm still not sure which of us was the whirlwind, though."

Cardynge scowled. His left hand clenched. "Bayard tried to warn me," he said. "Not that he knew her any too well. But he did know she was one of the—it isn't fashionable to call them beat any more, is it? The kind who spend most of their time hanging around in the coffee shops bragging about what they're going to do someday, and meanwhile cadging their living any way they can. Though that doesn't describe Lisette either. She turned out to have a good deal more force of character than that bunch. Anyhow, when he saw I was serious, Bayard begged me not to go any further with her. We had quite a fight about it. I married her a couple of days later."

Cardynge made a jerky sort of shrug. "Never mind the details," he said. "I soon learned she was a bitch on wheels. At first, after seeing what happened to our joint checking account, I thought she was simply extravagant. But what she said, and did, when I tried to put the brakes on her—! Now I'm mortally certain she didn't actually spend most of the money, but socked it away somewhere. I also know she had lovers. She taunted me with that, at the end.

"Before then she drove Bayard out. You can guess how many little ways there are to make a proud, sensitive young man unwelcome in his own father's house. Finally he exploded and told the truth about her, to both our faces. I still felt honor bound to defend her, at least to the extent of telling him to shut up or leave. 'Very well, I'll go,' he said, and that was the last I saw of him. Four months back. He simply left town."

"Have you heard anything from him since?" Yamamura asked.

"A short letter from Seattle, some while ago," Cardynge finished his cigarette and extracted a

fresh one. "Obviously trying to mend his friendship with me, if not her. He only said he was
okay, but the job he'd found was a poor one.
He'd heard of better possibilities elsewhere, so
he was going to go have a look and he'd write
again when he was settled. I haven't heard yet. I
tried to get his current address from his draft
board, but they said they weren't allowed to
release any such information. So I came to you."

"I see." Yamamura drew on his pipe. "Don't
worry too much, Mr. Cardynge. He sounds like
a good, steady kid, who'll land on his feet."

"Uh-huh. But I must locate him. You see,
Lisette and I separated month before last. Not
formally. We . . . we've even seen each other on
occasion. She can still be lovely in every way,
when she cares to. I've been sending her money,
quite a decent sum. But she says she wants to
come back."

"Do you want her yourself?"

"No. It's a fearful temptation, but I'm too
well aware of what the end result would be. So
she told me yesterday, if I didn't take her back,
she'd file for divorce. And you know what a
woman can do to a man in this state."

"Yeah."

"I'm quite prepared to make a reasonable
settlement," Cardynge said. "A man ought to
pay for his mistakes. But I'll be damned if I'll
turn over so much to her that it ruins the business my son was going to inherit."

"Um-m-m . . . are you sure he really wants
to?"

"I am. He was majoring in business administration on that account. But your question's a very natural one, though, which is also bound to occur to the courts. If Bayard isn't here at the trial, it won't seem as if he has much interest that needs protection. Also, he's the main witness to prove the, the mental cruelty wasn't mine. At least, not entirely mine—I think." Cardynge gestured savagely with his cigarette. "All right, I married a girl young enough to be my daughter. We look at life differently. But I tried to please her."

Yamamura liked him for the admission.

"I've no proof about the lovers," Cardynge said, "except what she told me herself in our last fight. And, well, indications. You know. Never mind, I won't ask anyone to poke into that. Lisette was nearly always charming in company. And I'm not given to weeping on my friends' shoulders. So, as I say, we need Bayard's testimony. If there's to be any kind of justice done. In fact, if we can get him back before the trial, I'm sure she'll pull in her horns. The whole wretched business can be settled quietly, no headlines, no—You understand?"

"I believe so." Yamamura considered him a while before asking gently, "You're still in love with her, aren't you?"

Cardynge reddened. Yamamura wondered if he was going to get up and walk out. But he slumped and said, "If so, I'll get over it. Will you take the case?"

The rest of the discussion was strictly ways and means.

*　　*　　*

Rain pursued Yamamura to the porch of the house. Right and left and behind was only blackness, the neighborhood slept. But here light spilled from the front windows, made his dripping coat shimmer and glistened on the spears that slanted past the rail. The wind howled too loudly for him to hear the doorbell.

But the man inside ought to—

Yamamura grew aware that he had stood ringing for well over a minute. Perhaps the bell was out of order. He seized the knocker and slammed it down hard, again and again. Nothing replied but the storm.

Damnation! He tried the knob. The door opened. He stepped through and closed it behind him. "Hello," he called. "Are you here, Mr. Cardynge?"

The whoop outside felt suddenly less violent than it was—distant, unreal, like that voice over the wire. The house brimmed with silence.

It was a big, old-fashioned house; the entry hall where he stood was only dully lit from the archway to the living room. Yamamura called once more and desisted. The sound was too quickly lost. *Maybe he went out, I'll wait.* He hung coat and hat on the rack and passed on in.

The room beyond, illuminated by a ceiling light and a floor lamp, was large and low, well furnished but with the comfortable slight shabbiness of a long-established home. At the far end was a couch with a coffee table in front.

Cardynge lay there.

Yamamura plunged toward him. "Hey!" he

shouted, and got no response. Cardynge was sprawled full length, neck resting across the arm of the couch. Though his eyes were closed, the jaw had dropped open and the face was without color. Yamamura shook him a little. The right leg flopped off the edge; its shoe hit the carpet with a thud that had no resonance.

Judas priest! Yamamura grabbed a horribly limp wrist. The flesh did not feel cold, but it yielded too much to pressure. He couldn't find any pulse.

His watch crystal was wet. On the table stood a nearly empty fifth of bourbon, a glass with some remnants of drink, and a large pill bottle. Yamamura reached out, snatched his fingers back— possible evidence there—and brought Cardynge's left arm to the mouth. That watch didn't fog over.

His first thought was of artificial respiration. Breath and heart could not have stopped very long ago. He noticed the dryness of the tongue, the uncleanliness elsewhere. *Long enough,* he thought, and rose.

The storm hurled itself against silence and fell back. In Yamamura's mind everything was overriden by the marble clock that ticked on the mantel, the last meaningful sound in the world. He had rarely felt so alone.

What had Cardynge said, in his call?

Yamamura started across the room to the telephone, but checked himself. Could be fingerprints. The police would soon arrive anyway, and there was no use in summoning a rescue squad which might be needed another place.

He returned to the body and stood looking down. Poor Cardynge. He hadn't appeared a suicidal type; but how much does any human know of any other? The body was more carefully dressed, in suit and clean shirt and tie, than one might have expected from a man baching it. Still, the room was neat too. Little more disturbed its orderliness than a couple of butts and matches in an ashtray on the end table next the couch. No day servant could maintain such conditions by herself.

Wait a bit. A crumpled sheet of paper, on the floor between couch and coffee table. Yamamura stopped, hesitated, and picked it up. Even dead, his client had a claim on him.

He smoothed it out with care. It had originally been folded to fit an envelope. A letter, in a woman's handwriting, dated yesterday.

My dear Aaron—

—for you were very dear to me once, and in a way you still are. Not least, I suppose, because you have asked me to return to you, after all the heartbreak and bitterness. And yes, I believe you when you swear you will try to make everything different between us this time. Will you, then, believe me when I tell you how long and agonizingly hard I have thought since we spoke of this? How it hurts me so much to refuse you that I can't talk of it, even over the phone, but have to write this instead?

But if I came back it would be the same hideous thing over again. Your temper, your inflexibility, your suspicion. Your son returning, as he will, and your inability to see how insanely he hates me for taking his mother's place, how he will work and work until he succeeds in poisoning your mind about me. And I'm no saint myself. I admit that. My habits, my outlook, my demands—am I cruel to say that you are too old for them?

No, we would only hurt each other the worse. I don't want that, for you or for myself. So I can't come back.

I'm going away for a while, I don't know where, or if I did know I wouldn't tell you, because you might not stop pleading with me and that would be too hard to bear. I don't want to see you again. Not for a long time, at least, 'til our wounds have scarred. I'll get an attorney to settle the business part with you. I wish you everything good. Won't you wish the same for me? Goodbye, Aaron.

Lisette

Yamamura stared into emptiness. *I wonder what she'll think when she learns what this letter drove him to do.*

She may even have counted on it.

He put the sheet back approximately as he had found it, and unconsciously wiped his fingers on his trousers. In his need to keep busy, he squatted to examine the evidence on the table. His nose was keen, he could detect a slight acridness in the smell about the glass. The bottle from the drugstore held sleeping pills prescribed for Cardynge. It was half empty. Barbiturates and alcohol can be a lethal combination.

And yet— Yamamura got to his feet. He was not unacquainted with death, he had looked through a number of its many doors and the teachings of the Buddha made it less terrible to him than to most. But something was wrong here. The sense of that crawled along his nerves.

Perhaps only the dregs of the nightmare from which Cardynge had roused him.

Yamamura wanted his pipe in the worst way. But better not smoke before the police had seen what was here . . . as a matter of form, if nothing else. Form was something to guard with great care, on this night when chaos ran loose beyond the walls and the world stood unmeasurably askew within them.

He began to prowl. A wastepaper basket was placed near the couch. Struck by a thought—his logical mind functioned swiftly and unceasingly, as if to weave a web over that which lay below— he crouched and looked in. Only two items. The housekeeper must have emptied the basket today, and Cardynge tossed these in after he got back from his office. He wouldn't have observed the holiday; few establishments did, and he would have feared leisure. Yamamura fished them out.

One was a cash register receipt from a local liquor store, dated today. The amount shown corresponded to the price of a fifth such as stood on the table. Lord, but Cardynge must have been drunk, half out of his skull, when he prepared that last draught for himself!

The other piece was an envelope, torn open

by hand, addressed here and postmarked yesterday evening in Berkeley. So he'd have found it in his mail when he came home this afternoon. In the handwriting of the letter, at the upper left corner, stood *Lisette Cardynge* and the apartment address her husband had given Yamamura.

The detective dropped them back into the basket and rose with a rather forced shrug. So what? If anything, this clinched the matter. One need merely feel compassion now, an obligation to find young Bayard—no, not even that, since the authorities would undertake it—so, no more than a wish to forget the whole business. There was enough harm and sorrow in the world without brooding on the unamendable affairs of a near stranger.

Only . . . Cardynge had wakened him, helplessly crying for help. And the wrongness would not go away.

Yamamura swore at himself. What was it that looked so impossible here? Cardynge's telephoning? He'd spoken strangely, even—or especially—for a man at the point of self-murder. *Though he may have been delirious. And certainly I was half asleep, in a morbid state, myself. I could have mixed his words with my dreams, and now be remembering things he never said.*

The suicide, when Cardynge read Lisette's ultimate refusal?

Or the refusal itself? Was it in character for her? Yamamura's mind twisted away from the room, two days backward in time.

*   *   *

He was faintly relieved when she came to his office. Not that the rights or wrongs of the case had much to do with the straightforward task of tracing Bayard and explaining why he should return. But Yamamura always preferred to hear both sides of a story.

He stood up as she entered. Sunlight struck through the window, a hurried shaft between clouds, and blazed on her blonde hair. She was tall and slim, with long green eyes in a singularly lovely face, and she walked like a cat. "How do you do?" he said. Her hand lingered briefly in his before they sat down, but the gesture looked natural. He offered her a cigaret from a box he kept for visitors. She declined.

"What can I do for you, Mrs. Cardynge?" he asked, with a little less than his normal coolness.

"I don't know," she said unhappily. "I've no right to bother you like this."

"You certainly do, since your husband engaged me. I suppose he is the one who told you?"

"Yes. We saw each other yesterday, and he said he'd started you looking for his son. Do you think you'll find him?"

"I have no doubts. The man I sent to Seattle called in this very morning. He'd tracked down some of Bayard's associates there, who told him the boy had gone to Chicago. No known address, but probably as simple a thing as an ad in the paper will fetch him. It's not as if he were trying to hide."

She stared out of the window before she swung

those luminous eyes back and said, "How can I get you to call off the search?"

Yamamura chose his words with care. "I'm afraid you can't. I've accepted a retainer."

"I could make that up to you."

Yamamura bridled. "Ethics forbid."

One small hand rose to her lips. "Oh, I'm so sorry. Please don't think I'm offering a bribe. But—" She blinked hard, squared her shoulders, and faced him head on. "Isn't there such a thing as a higher ethic?"

"Well-ll . . . what do you mean, Mrs. Cardynge?"

"I suppose Aaron praised Bayard at great length. And quite honestly, too, from his own viewpoint. His only son, born of his first wife, who must have been a dear person. How *could* Aaron see how evil he is?"

Yamamura made a production of charging his pipe. "I hear there was friction between you and the boy," he said.

A tired little smile tugged at her mouth. "You put it mildly. And of course I'm prejudiced. After all, he wrecked my marriage. Perhaps 'evil' is too strong a word. Nasty? And that may apply to nothing but his behavior toward me. Which in turn was partly resentment at my taking his mother's place, and partly—" Lisette stopped.

"Go on," said Yamamura, low.

Color mounted in her cheeks. "If you insist. I think he was in love with me. Not daring to admit it to himself, he did everything he could to get me out of his life. And out of his father's.

He was more subtle than a young man ought to be, though. Insinuations; provocations; disagreements carefully nursed into quarrels—" She gripped the chair arms. "Our marriage, Aaron's and mine, would never have been a simple one to make work. The difference in age, outlook, everything. I'm not perfect either, not easy to live with. But I was trying. Then Bayard made the job impossible for both of us."

"He left months ago," Yamamura pointed out.

"By that time the harm was done, even if he didn't realize it himself."

"Does it matter to you any more what he does?"

"Yes. I—Aaron wants me to come back." She looked quickly up. "No doubt he's told you otherwise. He has a Victorian sense of privacy. The sort of man who maintains appearances, never comes out of his shell, until at last the pressure inside gets too great and destroys him. But he's told me several times since I left that I can come back any time I want."

"And you're thinking of doing so?"

"Yes. Though I can't really decide. It would be hard on us both, at best, and nearly unbearable if we fail again. But I do know that Bayard's presence would make the thing absolutely impossible." She clasped her purse with a desperate tightness. "And even if I decide not to try, if I get a divorce, the lies Bayard would tell—Please, Mr. Yamamura! Don't make a bad matter worse!"

The detective struck match to tobacco and did not speak until he had the pipe going. "I'm sorry," he said. "But I can't decree that a father should not get in touch with his son. Even if I did resign from the case, he can hire someone else. And whatever happens, Bayard won't stay away forever. Sooner or later you'll have to face this problem. Won't you?"

The bright head bent. "I'm sorry," Yamamura said again.

She shook herself and jumped to her feet. "That's all right," she whispered. "I see your point. Of course. Don't worry about me. I'll manage. Thanks for your trouble." He could scarcely rise before she was gone.

The doorbell jarred Yamamura to awareness. As he opened for the patrolman, the storm screamed at him. "Hi, Charlie," he said in a mutter. "You didn't have a useless trip. Wish to hell you had."

Officer Moffat hung up his slicker. "Suicide?"

"Looks that way. Though—Well, come see for yourself."

Moffat spoke little before he had examined what was in the living room. Then he said, "Joe told me this was a client of yours and he called you tonight. What'd he want?"

"I don't know." Yamamura felt free, now, to console himself with his pipe. "His words were so incoherent, and I was so fogged with sleep myself, that I can't remember very well. Frankly, I'm just as glad."

"That figures for a suicide. Also the Dear John letter. What makes you so doubtful?"

Yamamura bit hard on his pipestem. The bowl

became a tiny campfire over which to huddle. "I can't say. You know how it is when you're having a dream, and something is gruesomely wrong but you can't find out what, only feel that it is? That's what this is like."

He paused. "Of course," he said, seeking rationality, "Cardynge and his wife told me stories which were somewhat inconsistent. She claimed to me he wanted her back; he denied it. But you know how big a liar anyone can become when his or her most personal affairs are touched on. Even if he spoke truth at the time, he could have changed his mind yesterday. In either case, he'd have gotten drunk when she refused in this note, and if it turned out to be an unhappy drunk he could have hit the absolute bottom of depression and killed himself."

"Well," Moffat said, "I'll send for the squad." He laid a handkerchief over the phone and put it to his ear. "Damn! Line must be down somewhere. I'll have to use the car radio."

Yamamura remained behind while the policeman grumbled his way back into the rain. His eyes rested on Cardynge's face. It was so recently dead that a trace of expression lingered, but nothing he could read. As if Cardynge were trying to tell him something. . . . The thought came to Yamamura that this house was now more alive than its master, for it could still speak.

Impulsively, he went through the inner door and snapped on the light. Dining room, with a stiff, unused look; yes, the lonely man doubtless ate in the kitchen. Yamamura continued thither.

That was a fair-sized place, in cheerful colors which now added to desolation. It was as neat as everything else. One plate, silverware, and coffee apparatus stood in the drainrack. They were dry, but a dishtowel hung slightly damp. Hm . . . Cardynge must have washed his things quite shortly before he mixed that dose. Something to do with his hands, no doubt, a last effort to fend off the misery that came flooding over him. Yamamura opened the garbage pail, saw a well-gnawed T-bone and the wrappers from packages of frozen peas and French fries. Proof, if any were needed, that Cardynge had eaten here, doubtless been here the whole time. The refrigerator held a good bit of food; one ice tray was partly empty. Yamamura went on to the bathroom and bedrooms without noticing anything special.

Moffat came back in as the other man regained the living room. "They're on their way," he said. "I'll stick around here. You might as well go on home, Trig."

"I suppose so." Yamamura hesitated. "Who'll notify his wife?"

Moffat regarded him closely. "You've met her, you said, and know something about the case. Think you'd be able to break the news gently?"

"I don't know. Probably not. Anyhow, looks as if I'll have to tell his son, when we find him."

Moffat tilted back his cap and rubbed his head. "Son left town? We'll have to interview him ourselves. To tie up loose ends, make sure he really was away and so forth. Not that—Huh?"

Yamamura picked his pipe off the floor.

"What's the matter, Trig?"

"Nothing." The detective wheeled about, stared at the body on the couch and then out the window into night.

"Uh, one thing," Moffat said. "Since you do know a little about her. Think we should notify Mrs. Cardynge at once, or let her sleep till morning?"

It yelled within Yamamura.

"I mean, you know, theoretically we should send someone right off," Moffat said, "but even if she has left him, this is going to be a blow. Especially since she's indirectly respon—"

Yamamura snatched Moffat's arm. "Yes!" he cried. "Right away! Can you get a man there this instant?"

"What?"

"To arrest her!"

"Trig, are you crazy as that stiff was?"

"We may already be too late. Get back to your radio!"

Moffat wet his lips. "What do you mean?"

"The purse. Hers. The evidence will be there, if she hasn't had time to get rid of it— By God, if you don't, I'll make a citizen's arrest myself!"

Moffat looked into the dilated eyes a full second before he pulled himself loose. "Okay, Trig. What's her address again?" Yamamura told him and he ran off without stopping to put on his coat.

Yamamura waited, pipe smoldering in his hand. A dark peace rose within him. The wrongness had departed. There was nothing here worse than a dead man and a night gone wild.

Moffat re-entered, drenched and shivering. "I had to give them my word I had strong presumptive evidence," he said. "Well, I know what you've done in the past. But this better be good."

"Good enough, if we aren't too late," Yamamura said. He pointed to the ashtray. "Cardynge was pretty nervous when he talked to me," he went on. "He hated to bare his soul. So he smoked one cigaret after another. But here—two butts for an entire evening. If you look in the kitchen, you'll find that he made a hearty meal. And washed up afterward. Does any of this square with a man utterly shattered by a Dear John letter?

"The dishes are dry in the rack. But something was washed more recently. The towel is still moist, even thought the saliva has dried in the corpse's mouth. What was washed? And by whom?"

Moffat grew rigid. "You mean that letter's a plant? But the envelope—"

"Something else was in that envelope. 'Dear Aaron, can I come see you tonight on a very private matter? Lisette.' She came with a pretext for discussion that could not have been particularly disturbing to him. Nor could her presence have been; his mind was made up about her. But they had a few drinks together.

"At some point she went to the bathroom, taking her glass along, and loaded it with powder poured from the capsules. Then, I'd guess, while he went, she switched glasses with him. She'd know he used sleeping pills. Convenient for her. Still, if he had not, she could have gotten some other poison without too much trouble or danger.

"Of course, she couldn't be sure the dose would prove fatal, especially since I doubt if they drank much. Maybe she patted his head, soothed him, so he drifted into unconsciousness without noticing. He'd take a while, possibly an hour or two, to die. She must have waited, meanwhile arranging things. Washed both glasses that had her prints on them, fixed the one on the table here and clasped his hand around it for prints and poured most of the whiskey down the sink.

"If he'd started coming around, she could have returned the pill bottle to the bathroom and told him he'd had a fainting spell or whatever. She could even say she'd tried to get a doctor, but none could or would come. He wouldn't be suspicious. As things turned out, though, he died and she left. The only thing she overlooked was the evidence of the food and cigarets."

Moffat tugged his chin. "The autopsy will show how much he did or did not drink," he said. "Did that occur to her?"

"Probably. But it's no solid proof. He didn't *have* to be on a tear when he decided to end his life. The missing booze could've been spilled accidentally. But it would help plant the idea of suicide in people's minds. She's clever. Ruthless. And one hell of a fine actress."

"Motive?"

"Money. If Bayard testified against her in the divorce proceedings, she'd get nothing but the usual settlement. But as a widow, she'd inherit a mighty prosperous business. She married him in the first place for what she could get out of him, of course."

Moffat clicked his tongue. "I'd hoped for better than this from you, Trig," he said with a note of worry. "You're really reaching."

"I know. This is more hunch than anything else. There won't even be legal grounds for an indictment, if she's disposed of the proof."

"Do you suppose she was mistaken about his being dead, and after she left he roused himself long enough to call you? That sounds unlikeliest of all."

"No argument," said Yamamura grimly. "That call's the one thing I can't explain."

They fell silent, amidst the rain and wind and relentless clock-tick, until the homicide squad arrived. The first officer who came in the door looked pleased, in a bleak fashion. "We got the word on our way here," he said. "She wasn't home, so the patrolman waited. She arrived a few minutes afterward."

"Must have left this house—" Yamamura looked at his watch. 2:27. Had the whole thing taken so short a while? "About an hour ago, seeing I was phoned then. Even in this weather, that's slow driving."

"Why, no. She said twenty minutes or thereabouts."

"What? You're sure? How do you know?"

"Oh, she broke down and confessed all over the place, as soon as Hansen asked where she'd been and looked in her purse."

Yamamura let out his breath in a long, shaken sigh.

"What was there?" Moffat asked.

"The original note, which asked for this meeting and furnished an envelope to authenticate the fake one," Yamamura said. "I was hoping she'd taken it back with her, to destroy more thoroughly than she might have felt safe in doing here." More sadness than victory was in his tone: "I admit I'm surprised she spilled her guts so fast. But it must have affected her more than she'd anticipated, to sit and watch her husband die, with nothing but that clock speaking to her."

The discrepancy hit him anew. He turned to the homicide officer and protested: "She can't have left here only twenty minutes ago. That's barely before my arrival. Cardynge woke me almost half an hour before that!"

"While she was still here—?" Moffat contemplated Yamamura for a time that grew long. "Well, he said at length, "maybe she'd gone to the can." He took the phone. "We just might be able to check that call, if we hurry."

"The line's dead," Yamamura reminded him.

"No, I get a dial tone now," Moffat said. "They must've repaired it a few minutes ago. Hello, operator—"

Yamamura became occupied with explaining his presence and showing the squad around. When they came back to the living room, Moffat had cradled the phone. He stood so unmoving that their own feet halted.

"What's the matter, Charlie?" the inspector asked. "You look like the devil. Couldn't you find out anything?"

"No." Moffat shook his head, slowly, as if it weighed too much. "There wasn't any call."

"What?" Yamamura exclaimed.

"You heard me," Moffat said. "This line went down about midnight. Wasn't fixed 'til now." He took a step forward. "Okay, Trig. What really brought you here?"

"A phone call, I tell you." Yamamura's back ached with a tension he could not will away. "From Cardynge."

"And I tell you that's impossible."

Yamamura stood a while hearing the clock tick. Finally, flatly, he said: "All right. Maybe there never was a call. I was half asleep, half awake, my brain churning. I guess that subconsciously I was worried about Cardynge, and so I dreamed the message, even took the phone off the rack, it felt so real."

"Well . . . yes." Moffat began to relax. "That must be what happened. Funny coincidence, though."

"It better be a coincidence," Yamamura said.

The men looked simultaneously at the body, and at the phone, and away.

—Poul and Karen Anderson

BELA LUGOSI

1883 - 1956

Do you remember how he gave the sharp
Kiss of undeath, and how he wrapped the
  night
Of his cloak about white Mina? And do you
Remember how we tingled at the nape
When we saw his face, and saw his wilful smile?
We loved his voice, his eyes that held our own
While a taut coldness took us by the throat;
We kept our secret thoughts of his high head
So proudly held—his arrogance of grace.

Then we could understand why legends told
Of demons' beauty, and named "Bearer of Light"
Him who for pride had cloaked himself with
  Hell.

—Karen Anderson

THE KITTEN

The flames roared. They stood aloft from the house in cataracts of red, yellow, hell-blue, which a breeze made ragged and cast as a spray of sparks against cold November stars. Their blaze roiled in smoke, flashed off neighbor windows, sheened over the snow that lay thin upon lawns and banked along hedges. Meltwater around burning walls had boiled off, and grass beneath was charred. The heat rolled forth like a tide. Men felt it parch their eyeballs and stood back from trying to breast it. Meanwhile it strewed reek around them.

Blink, blink went the turret light on the fire chief's car. Standing beside it, he and the police chief could oversee his trucks. Paint and metal gleamed through darkness, background for men who sluiced thick white jets out of hoses. Hoarse shouts seemed remote, nearly lost amidst boom and brawl. Still farther away were the spectators, a shadow mass dammed in the street to right and left by a few officers. And the view downhill, of Senlac's lamps and homes in peaceful arrays, the river frozen among them, a glimpse of grey-white farmland beyond, could have been on a planet circling in Orion.

"Yeah, about as bad as they come," said the fire chief. His breath made each word a ghostly explosion. "We just hope we can keep it from spreading next door. I guess we can."

"Damn, there goes any evidence," said the police chief. He slapped arms over chest. The fury he watched did not radiate very far.

"Well, we might find something in the ashes," said the fire chief. "Though I should think whatever you can use is in, uh, the other place."

"Probably," said the police chief. "Still . . . I dunno. On the face of it, the case looks open and shut. But what I've heard tonight— I've seen my share of weirdos, not only when I was on the force in Chicago, Jim, but here in our quiet, smallish Midwestern town too, oh, yes. And this business doesn't fit any pattern. It smells all wrong."

Brroomm, went the flames. *Rao-ow-ow. Sssss.*

Leo Tronen's wife made no scene when she left him. She deemed they had had enough of those in the three years they were married, culminating in the one the evening before. That was when he stormed into her study, snatched her half-written thesis off the desk, brought it back to the living room, tossed it in the grate,

and snapped his cigarette lighter to the strewn
paper. As he rose, he spoke softly: "Does this
convince you?"

For an instant Una flinched away. An odd
little breaking noise came out of her throat. She
was a short woman, well formed, features deli-
cately boned, eyes blue and huge, nose tip-tilted,
lips forever a bit parted, face framed between
wings of blonde hair. And Tronen loomed six
feet three, and had been a football star at his
university. Then she clenched fists, stood her
ground, and whispered almost wonderingly, "You
would do such a thing. You really would. I kept
praying we could work our troubles out—"

"Jesus Christ, haven't I tried?" His voice
loudened. "A million times at least. From practically the first day we met, I explained— I don't
need a college professor—an Egyptologist, for
God's sake!—I need a wife."

She shook her head. "No." Soundless tears
coursed forth. "You need, want, a status symbol.
A mirror." She wheeled and walked from him.
He heard her shoes on the stairs, and how she
fought her sobs.

Ordinarily Tronen drank no more than his
work required, including, of course, necessary
cocktail parties. Now he put down a fair amount
of Scotch before he too went to bed, thinking
how magnanimous he was in taking the guest
room. That would be a point to make tomorrow,
when he must take the lead in cleaning up the
chaos that had overcome their relationship. For
instance: "Be honest. The main reason we don't
have a better sex life is you're still stuck on that

Quarters character. I realize you don't admit it
to yourself, but you are. Okay, you dated him in
college, and you both like to talk about countries dead and gone, and maybe my action yesterday was too extreme. If so, I'm sorry. But
don't you see, I had to do something to make
you understand how you've been letting me
down? What is Harry Quarters? A high school
history teacher! And what use to you, to us,
would your precious master's degree be, that
you're making a forty-mile commute three days
a week to study for? You're an executive's wife,
my dear, and we're bound for the top. You'll
visit your Pyramids in style—if you'll help out!"

She wasn't awake when his alarm clock rang.
At least, the bedroom door was closed. Frostily
indignant, he made his own breakfast and drove
off into a dim false dawn. Hadn't he *told* her he
must rise early today? He'd be showing the man
from John Deere around, which could result in
a seven-figure subcontract, which could get Leo
Tronen promoted out of this hole.

He was a country boy by origin, but had the
lights of New York in his eyes. His corporate
employer had made him the manager of a die-
cutting plant it had built outside Senlac, where
land was cheap. "A fine opening, especially for
a young fellow like you," they told him. But he
saw the blind alley beyond. You can only go so
far, producing stuff people actually use. The real
money, prestige, power lie in operating the people themselves and the paper which governs
them. Well, let him make a good showing here—

much more important, let the right men know
he did—and he'd get the big offer.

However, for this the right wife was essential:
attractive, alert, intelligent, skillful as hostess
or as guest. And he had reached Senlac newly
divorced. He met Una Nyborg at a party, zeroed
in and, being a handsome redhead with a quick
tongue and some sophistication, succeeded before long. She lived near Holberg College then,
pursuing graduate studies which he agreed she
might continue on a part-time basis after they
were married. He didn't expect she would for
many months. He had shown her such dazzling
visions of wonderful places and wonderful persons they would meet all over the world. At
first, when she nonetheless persisted in her private undertaking, he was annoyed. Later, when
it became inconvenient for him, sometimes an
out-and-out business handicap, he grew angry.

At last—enough was enough. Una simply must
straighten out and fly right. He'd start seeing to
that this very day after work.

Dusk was falling when he came home. There
were no street lamps in this new residential
district, and windows glowed well apart, pick-
ing out bare trees and a crust of old snow. The
air was hushed and raw. The tires of his Cadil-
lac made a susurrus that was nearly the single
sound. His multiglassed split-level stood dark.
Nothing but an automatically opened door and
lit bulb in the garage welcomed him. Una's Morris Minor was gone.

What the devil? He let himself in at the main
entrance and switched on lights as he passed

through the hall beyond. Long, wide, creamy of walls and drapes, thick and blue of carpet, Swedish modern of furniture, equipped with fieldstone fireplace and picture window, less militarily neat than he desired, the living room felt somehow emptier than the garage, somehow colder in spite of a heating system that mumbled like the ghosts of important visitors he had entertained here.

Was Una off shopping? A strange hour, but she was poorly organized at best, and doubtless distraught after last night's showdown. An envelope propped against a table lamp caught his glance. He strode to investigate. *"Leo"* said her handwriting. Fear stabbed him. He snatched a paperknife and ripped. The sheet within was covered by her scrawl, worse than usual, here and there water-blotted. He read twice before he grasped the meaning.

". . . can't go on . . . think I still love you, but . . . no alimony or anything . . . please don't try to find me, I'll call in a few days when this isn't hurting so hard. . . ."

"Why, how could she?" he heard himself say. "After all I've done for her."

Savagely he crumpled note and envelope, tossed them in the grate across the remnants of her thesis, sought the liquor cabinet and poured a stiff slug, flung himself onto the couch, popped lighter to cigarette, and dragged in a lungful.

What an absolute hell of a moment for her to desert. Where could she be? He mustn't make frantic inquiries. Discretion, yes, that was the word, heal the breach behind the scenes or at least finalize it inconspicuously. But could he trust her not to make a fool of him? If she'd sought shelter from a friend . . . No, hardly that. She'd likeliest gone to the city and entered a hotel under an assumed name. She was dreamy but not idiotic, unstable (Quarters—and now this!) but not disloyal. What had she said, during a recent quarrel? "You keep a good man locked away behind your ego. I know. You've sometimes let him out . . . on a chain, but out, to me, and he's who I love. Oh, Leo, give him a chance. Let him go free." Some such slush. Quite possibly she hoped her action would force a reconciliation.

His first drink went down in two consecutive cigarettes' worth of time. He fetched a refill and sipped more calmly. A sense of thaw spread through him. Una had told him how the ancient— Persians, were they? —always debated vital matters twice before deciding, drunk and sober. He smiled. Not that he meant to tie one on. However . . . He wasn't a monster of selfishness, nor narrow, really. He saw the reason for Una's interests; yes, he had felt a tug of the same when she talked. If only he had leisure . . . Unfair to call her ungrateful. She had in fact tried hard, though being helpmate to his kind of man didn't come natural. Had he for his part been less tolerant, less giving, even, than he ought? Could he rise as far in the world, no doubt slower but as far in the long run, if he relaxed more with her while they were still young?

Let her make her gesture. If an acquaintance asked where she was, say she'd gone out of town on a visit. When she contacted him, let them discuss matters in a reasonable way.

And let him rustle together a meal before he got loaded. Tronen chuckled rather sadly and went to the kitchen. She'd cleaned his breakfast dishes. That touched him; he wasn't sure why, but it did.

He had selected a can of corned beef hash when he heard a noise. In the stillness which engulfed him, he stood startled. The noise came again, a weak mew . . . Stray cat? He shrugged. A third cry sounded. He'd better check. The window above the sink was so full of darkness.

When he opened the kitchen door that gave on the patio, light spilled into a thick blue-brown gloom which quickly swallowed it. Thus the kitten on the stoop crouched all alone in his sight. It was about three months old, a bundle of white fur fluffed out against the chill, a pink nose, two large amber eyes. *"Weep,"* it piped, *"weep,"* and bounded past him into the warmth behind.

"Hey, wait a minute," Tronen said. The kitten sat on the linoleum and looked up at him, up, up, up. It didn't appear starved or ill. Then why had it invaded his house?

Tronen bent over to take the beast and put it back out. It ran from his hand, huddled in a corner by the stove, and watched him as if terrified. Why should a pet be afraid of a man? Tronen felt the night reach in, icy around his backbone. He sighed, rose, closed the door. The creature must have gotten lost. On those short legs, it couldn't have wandered far. Okay, he'd give it a place till he'd eaten, then phone around and learn whose it was. Several of his neighbors were prominent in Senlac, two of them—a state party committeeman and the owner of a growing grocery chain—on a larger scale. His kindliness would be appreciated. He hoped the kitten was housebroken.

Minutes later, as a pan sputtered savory smells, he heard another mew. The kitten had crept timidly forth to tell him it was hungry. Ah, well, why not oblige? On impulse, he warmed the milk; this was such a bleak night. The kitten assaulted the bowl ravenously. Tronen took a bench in the dinette for his own supper. After a bit, full-bellied, the kitten rubbed against his ankles. He reached down in an absentminded fashion and tickled softness. The kitten went into ecstasies. He resumed eating. The kitten sprang to his lap and curled in a ball. He felt the purr.

Having finished, he put the animal back on the floor. He meant to shut it in the kitchen, where misbehavior wouldn't have serious consequences, while he investigated. But it pattered by him too fast. "Damn!" It led him a merry chase to the living room. There it turned, sprang in his direction, rolled around at his feet, eager for fun and games.

Hm, he'd better determine the sex anyway. He settled on the couch again, by a phone he kept there (as well as those in the bedroom and his den). The kitten didn't mind examination. Male. He let his left hand keep it amused while his right dialed and his shoulder held the receiver.

Presently it snuggled alongside his thigh and licked his fingers, a tiny rasp with a motor going like crazy.

"—nice of you to call, Mr. Tronen, but we don't have cats. Have you tried the de Lanceys? I know they do."

"—present and accounted for here. Thanks a lot, though. Few people these days would bother."

"—not ours. But say, why don't you and your wife come have a drink one evening soon?"

He was sorry when he ran out of names. The house was too God damn silent. Not as much as a clock tick; on the mantel the minutes flickered by in digital readout. Music? No, he had a tin ear; the expensive hi-fi and record library were part of his image, and he wasn't about to fetch the ballads and jazz she enjoyed from Una's empty study. Television? What was on? Abruptly he remembered reading about single persons, especially old persons, in big cities, who grow so lonely that they kiss the faces on the screen. He shivered and turned his gaze elsewhere.

The kitten slept. Good idea for him. No more booze; a bromide, make that two bromides, eight or nine solid hours in the sack, and he'd be fit for work regardless of his problems. What about the kitten? It could hardly help letting go sometime during the night. He didn't fancy scrubbing a mess before he'd had coffee. But if he put the little wretch out, it'd freeze to death. He grinned at his indecision. Assign an engineer . . . In the garage was a beer case. He removed empty deposit bottles, took the box inside, added a layer of clean rags, set it by the stove, fetched the still bonelessly slumbering kitten, and shut the lid. On the point of departure, he suddenly added a fresh bowl of milk.

Upstairs, he threshed long awake, unhelped by his pills. Absurd, how his thoughts kept straying from Una, from the Deere contract, from everything real, to that silly infant animal. Probably he should put an ad in the paper. But then he could be stuck with the beast for days . . . The pound? . . . Una had always wished they'd keep a pet, specifically a cat. She'd accepted his veto. Now, a peace offering? Maybe he should experiment while she was gone, learn if the nuisance actually was intolerable . . . In his eventual sleep, a leopard stalked him.

His alarm clock brought him struggling to wakefulness. For a moment the dark before dawn was still full of shapes. He groped about; his palm closed on hair and warmth. *Una!* went through him like a sunbeam. Why was he gladdened? . . . No, wait, she was gone . . . Had she come back in the night? He fumbled overhead, found and yanked a reading lamp cord. On the pillow beside him rested the kitten.

Oh, no.

It regarded him brightly, pounced on his chest, patted his cheek with a fluff of paw. He sat straight, spilling it. Snatching for a hold, it clawed his neck. He swatted it aside. "Bloody pest!" Evidently he'd forgotten to reclose the lid of the box. He ached from restless hours. His skull was full of sand that gritted out through the eyesockets. As he left the bed, he noticed white smears on spread and electric blanket.

Suspicious, he sniffed. Uh-huh. Sour. The stinker must have upset the bowl from the kitchen, which itself must be a pool.

The kitten had retreated to a corner of the room. Its stare seemed hurt, not physically but in an eerily human fashion. Well, cats were a creepy breed. He'd never liked them.

Downstairs, he found his guess confirmed, and had to spend time with a mop before he could take care of his own needs. At least there was no piddle or dropping—Unh, he'd doubtless find some later, crusted in a place hard to get at. "Okay, chum," he said when the kitten appeared. "That settles the matter." It buzzed and tried to be petted. Behavior which had been slightly pleasant in his loneliness of yesterday was only irritating now.

Coffee and toast improved his mood. When he sought his car, the air seared him with a cold which had been deepening throughout the night. Silence crackled. Skeleton trees outlined against a sky turning from grey to bloodless white in the east were as stark a sight as he remembered ever seeing. For an instant he wondered if he ought to abandon the kitten in such weather.

At the back of his mind, the dream-leopard smiled.

He winced, grimaced, and lifted anger for a shield. What was he supposed to do? Be damned if he'd have this mess machine in his house any longer; and the pound would hardly commence business till nine or ten o'clock, by which time he must be well into the paperwork that the Deere representative had caused him to fall behind on; and— Somebody would find the creature and do something. Or if not, too many stray cats and dogs were running loose.

Thus the kitten sat on the front seat by him when he drove off, happy till he stopped, several miles from home, opened the right door, and tossed the animal out. It landed on its feet, unhurt though squeaking dismay. The sidewalk must indeed be frigid this morning, hard, barren. Beyond reached a municipal park, snowcrust, leafless boughs, benches like fossil monsters.

The kitten headed back for the car. "Oh, no, you don't," Thonen growled. He slammed the door, refastened his safety belt, and took off fast. His rear view mirror showed him a forlorn spot on the pavement; then soon that was gone.

"Nuts, I did more than could be expected," he said under his breath. What a miserable day. The chill had struck into his bones. Blast from the heater passed across him, useless as the first wan sunlight outside. "When I've got a tough job, and my wife's quit on me, and nobody gives an honest shit whether I live or die—"

No, wait, he told himself, don't whine. And don't be unrealistic. You matter to several people, at least. Your superiors want you where you are, fattening their bank accounts; your subordinates want you gone, out of the way of their advancement. It's forever Number One. Or Number Una? I thought I had an oasis of warmth in her, but she only wanted support while she sifted the dust of people three thousand years cold in death.

To hell with her. Let's see, this is Wednesday.

Saturday—I can wait till then, I'm not hot now, busy as I am—I'll run up to the city, a massage parlor, yeah, a straightforward transaction, cash for sex. "Cold as a whore's heart," the saying goes. Why not? Next time around, I'll marry more carefully.

The plant bulked like a squared-off glacier, its parking lot a moraine where as yet few cars were piled. Tronen hurried to the main door. The night watchman said, "Good morning, sir," in a mechanical tone, different from his usual heartiness. For a second Tronen thought: What ails Joe? Problems too? I should take time to ask—No. He doesn't care about me, does he?

The corridors hollowly echoed his footfalls. His office, paneled and picture-hung by specialists, seemed more hospitable at first. Then its stillness got to him and, for some ridiculous reason, the icicles that hung from a window frame. He turned the thermostat higher. When he settled back at his desk, the papers crackled in his fingers till he thought of frozen puddles underfoot.

"Good morning, Mr. Tronen," said his secretary when she arrived at nine. "My! Downright tropical in here."

"What?" He blinked at her trimness. "I'm comfortable," he said. That wasn't quite true; he still was wearing the jacket he normally discarded when working solo.

She went to the thermometer. "Eighty degrees?" Catching his glare: "Whatever you say, Mr. Tronen. I'm mostly beyond your door anyway, of course. But—excuse me—do you feel well? You look awfully tired."

"I'll do," he grunted. "Here," handing her a sheaf, "answer these according to my notes. I want the letters in the noon mail pickup."

"Yes, sir." Though respectful, she seldom used that honorific. Had he rebuffed her? Who cared?

His chief of operations came in at midmorning. "Uh, Leo, the John Deere man—not Gustafson; Kruchek, who Gustafson reports to, you remember—he was just on the line. And the questions he was asking about our quality control procedures . . . Well, I don't know about that subcontract now, Leo. I don't."

The union steward came in at midafternoon. "Mr. Tronen, you've explained to me how inflation means we've got to cut corners, and I guess I sympathize, and I've passed your word on to the boys. But the heating in the shop is inadequate. This'll likely be a dog-cold winter, and if you postpone making good on your promise to replace the whole system, I'm afraid you'll have a strike on your hands."

In between, while he lunched at his desk on a sandwich sent up from the cafeteria, the television brought him a newscast. Some government spokesmen admitted the country was already in a recession, and a few dared hint at an outright depression to come. Experts predicted a fuel shortage that would make last year's feel like a Hawaiian holiday.

Driving home through twilight, he recalled the kitten. He'd been too busy for that, throughout this day when trouble after trouble thrust at him and never a moment came to ease off and swap a bit of inconsequential friendship. Not that anybody had made overtures to him; he had no friends. Puss, he thought, whatever's happened to you this past ten or a dozen hours, be you alive or be you dead, you don't know what coldness is.

The garage machinery greeted him. He walked around to his front door. On the mat, a white blur, barely visible in dusk, was the kitten.

"What!" Tronen jumped back, off the porch, onto frozen snow beneath frozen stars. His heart lurched. Sweat prickled forth. This wasn't possible.

After a minute's harsh breath, he mastered the fear that he knew was irrational. He, scared of a nasty whimpering piece of flesh? If anything, *that* was the fact which should worry him. He advanced. The shape at his shoes barely stirred, barely mewed. He unlocked the door, reached around and switched on the porch light, squatted for a closer look. Yes, this was the same animal, though dreadfully weakened by cold and hunger, eyes dim, frost in fur and whiskers.

Cats come back. This one had simply had more staying power than was reasonable.

Tronen straightened. Under no circumstances would he let the thing inside, even for a single night. He wondered why he felt such loathing. At first he hadn't minded, and as for messiness, he could take due precautions. However . . . Ah, damn, he decided, I can't be bothered, with everything else I've got to plague me. Una would get sticky sentimental, but I—

The thought of having to dispose of an ice-hard corpse in the morning was distasteful. Tronen collected his will. He'd take care of the matter right now.

In the garage he fetched a bucket, which he filled from an outside tap. The metal of the faucet bit him with chill, the water rushed forth with a somehow horrible sound, a noise in this night like the flow of the Styx. He set his teeth, brought the bucket under the porch light, removed overcoat and jacket, rolled back his sleeves. The kitten stirred where it lay, as if trying to rise and lick his fingers. Hastily he plunged the small form under.

He hadn't known the squirming would go on so long. When at last he grasped stillness, it was as if something squirmed yet in his brain.

Or swirled, roiled, made a maelstrom? God, but he needed a drink! He fished out the body, laid it down, sloshed forth the water—a cataract, dim to see, loud to hear. Worst was to take the sodden object again, fumble around the far side of the garage, toss it into a garbage can and clatter the lid in place. When he had returned the bucket he hurried indoors to the nearest bathroom, flicking on every light along the way. There he washed his hands under the hottest stream they could endure.

Why was he squeamish? He'd never been before. His head felt wrong in every respect, dizzy and darkened, as if he were being sucked around and down in a whirlpool.

Well, he was short on sleep, and Una's desertion had maybe been more of a shock than he realized; and what about that drink?

At the liquor cabinet—how loudly Scotch gurgled out across ice. Tronen bore the glass to his easy chair. His grip shook till cubes chinked together and liquid splashed. The taste proved unappealing, and he had a crazy fear that he might send a swallow down the wrong throat and choke to death. Could be I've been mistaken to oppose legalizing marijuana, he thought through torrents. A relaxer that isn't liquid . . .

The phone shrilled. He jerked. The tumbler flew free, whisky rivered across the carpet, ice promptly began making brooks. Una? He stumbled to snatch the receiver. "Hello, who's this?" amidst wild waters.

"Harry Quarters here," said a male voice. "Hi, Leo. How are you?"

Tronen choked on a gob of saliva and coughed. But meanwhile he might almost have had a picturephone: before him stood yonder teacher, tall, bespectacled, rumple-clothed, diffident, pipe-sucking, detestable. The picturephone wasn't working right; the image wavered like a stone seen at the bottom of a rapid stream.

"Anything wrong, Leo?" Was that anxious note genuine? Hardly.

"No, nothing," Tronen overcame his spasm.

"Uh, could I speak to Una, please?"

A waterfall thundered. "What do you want with her?"

Taken aback by the loud response, Quarters stammered, "Why, why, to tell her about a book

I found in the city this weekend . . . Out of print,
but I think of interest to her for her research—"

"She's not home," Tronen snapped. "Visiting.
An extended visit."

"Oh." Quarters's surprise suggested that he
had expected she'd mention her plans to him.
"Where, may I ask? How long?"

Tronen hung onto self-control as if it were a
piece of flotsam. "A relative. Several days at
least."

"Oh." After a pause: "Well, you know. if we're
both baching, why don't we get together? Let
me take you out to dinner. Lord knows you've
had me over often enough."

Una has. "No," said Tronen. "I'm busy. Thanks."
He crashed the receiver onto the hook.

Briefly, then, he wondered why he had refused.
Company might be welcome, might be advisable.
And Quarters wasn't actually too bad a guy.
His conversation ranged well beyond Una's
Egyptology into areas like politics and sports
that interested her husband more; the man was
active in the former on the envelope-stuffing
level, and as for the latter, in high school he'd
been a star baseball pitcher and still played on
a YMCA team. Probably he was in love with
Una, but there was no reason to suppose he'd
ever tried anything untoward. In fact, if Tronen
led the conversation cleverly enough, helpful
information about her might develop . . . No. He
couldn't be clever when he felt afloat, awirl,
asink. And the thought of the dial tone if he
called back, that rushing *ng-ng-ng*, was grisly.

Maybe another day. He'd better mop up his

spilled drink before it soaked through the carpet. He decided against a replacement, cooked and bolted whatever was handiest in cans, found that neither newspaper nor television would register on him, and went to bed as early as seemed practical. First he took three sleeping pills.

His mind spiraled down and down into fluid blackness. For a while he gasped, struggled back, broke surface and panted air into his lungs. But the tide drew him again, again, until at last his strength was spent and he lay on the bottom, the weight of the ocean upon him, and knew for a thousand years that he was dead.

When the alarm rescued him, his pajamas were sodden with sweat. Nevertheless, the last thing he wanted was a shower. He shuddered his way out of the room, brain still submerged in his nightmare, barely able to think that a lot of coffee might help. The stairs cascaded away from the landing, dangerous; he clutched the bannister as he waded their length. When he reached the kitchen, his bare feet splatted on cold linoleum.

"*Weep,*" he heard beyond the door, "*weep, weep.*"

Did his hand turn the knob and heave of itself? Merciless light flooded forth. The kitten sprawled on the stoop. Drenched fur clung so tightly to its skin that it resembled a rat.

"No," Tronen heard himself gurgle, "no, no."

He grasped after sanity. He'd not held the horrible thing long enough under, it had revived, the air had warmed to above freezing, he'd not fitted the lid properly on the trash can either, during the darkness it had crawled over the rubbish inside till it escaped, while he drowned in his dream. . . .

This time, he thought somewhere, I'll do the job right.

He stooped, clutched feebly struggling sliminess, raised the slight weight, bashed head against concrete. He felt as well as heard a splintering crack. When he let go, the kitten lay motionless, save that blood trickled from pink nose and past tiny teeth. The amber eyes glazed over.

Tronen rose. The breath sucked in and out of him. He trembled.

But it was from excitement, anger, release. His delirium had left him. His mind felt sharp and clean as an ax. Catharsis, he thought, underneath, catharsis, is that the word? Whatever, I'm free.

He rejoiced to carry the body back to the garbage and, this time, ring down the lid loud enough to wake Harry Quarters across town. He scrubbed the blood and rinsed the sponge with a sense of having gotten back some of his own. Oh, he wasn't a child, he thought in the shower which he had become glad to take. He didn't blame the kitten personally. It had merely happened along at foul hours. In his confusion, subconscious mind on a rampage and all that stuff, he'd made the creature a symbol. Now he was done. He could cope with reality, the real people and real forces ranged against him. And would, by God! He hardly needed coffee. Wakefulness, anger sang in his veins.

His car leaped into the street. He fumed at the need to observe speed limits in more crowded areas where an officious cop might see him. *Why* couldn't a leading responsible private citizen, who had urgent business on which a substantial payroll depended, be allowed a siren to clear his path?

The watchman at the plant looked surly. No doubt he was a sympathizer of the machinists and their strike threat. How in Christ's name could a man explain the reasons, the elementary economics, behind an executive decision? Sure, the shop was chilly; but their workday ended after a measured eight hours (not that they honestly produced for half that time), unlike his which had no end. And meanwhile, was it impossible for them to wear heavier clothes? Could they absolutely not see that their jobs, their well-being was tied in to the company's? . . . No, they couldn't, because in fact that was not true. Let the company fail and they'd suck unemployment pay out of his taxes.

Management and capital didn't breed any race of angels either. In his office, Tronen hunched over papers which made him pound the desk till his fist was sore. What did that Kruchek mean, doubting the quality control here? What the hell did he expect? Gustafson had acted satisfied. Kruchek must have a private motive—unless Gustafson had led him on for reasons that would be very, very interesting to know . . . And this letter from the regional manager, the veiled complaints and demands, how was Tronen supposed to answer those, how much ass must a man kiss to get anywhere in this rotten system? No wonder it bred radicals and rioters! And then the authorities were too busy pussyfooting to do what was necessary: open fire on a few of those mobs.

His secretary was almost an hour late. "I'm sorry, my car wouldn't start—"

"It would not occur to you to call a taxi, of course, nor to make up the time. Didn't you mention once that you're a Lutheran? Ah, well, I suppose your keeping a Protestant work ethic was too much to hope for." He spoke levelly, reducing her to tears in lieu of the three or four slaps across the chops that the stupid cow deserved.

In midmorning he summoned his chief of operations. They were bothered by occasional juvenile vandalism in their isolated location, rocks through windows a few times a year, most recently naughty words painted on a wall. "I've about decided we need more guards for nights and holidays," he said. "Issue them shotguns— for use, not show."

"Huh?" The man recovered. "You're joking."

"Oh, we'd post conspicuous notices. And a single young hoodlum shot in the belly should end that form of recreation."

"Leo, do you feel all right? We can't use extreme violence—on kids—to prevent a few dollars' worth of damage. Anyhow, you objected yourself, when we discussed this before, that a chain link fence would cost out of proportion. Have you figured the wages of those extra guards?"

Tronen yielded. He had no choice. However, the law did not yet forbid him to sit half an hour and visualize what ought to be done.

The noontime newscast informed him that Arabs and Israelis had exchanged a fresh round of massacres. War seemed thoroughly possible. Well, he thought, let's get in there, fast, beat those bedouins to their flea-bitten knees, and assure our oil supplies. The Russians will scream, but they won't act if we catch them by surprise and keep SAC on red alert. Or if they are crazy enough to act, we'll survive, most of us. They won't.

The afternoon was pissed away on a sales engineer from a firm interested in redoing his heating system. No matter argument, the fellow wouldn't reduce his estimate to a figure that would please the home office and thus help get Tronen out of Senlac. Greedy bastard—on behalf of his employers, true, but his was the smug fat face which must be confronted more or less courteously, while inside, Tronen imagined kicking out those teeth and grinding a boot across that nose.

He left early. His stomach had become a cauldron of acid and he wasn't accomplishing anything. Thus daylight lingered when he got home, the sun a blood clot barely above the snowfields it tinged, long shadows of houses like bludgeons and of trees like knives. The cold and the silence had teeth. Judas, but the place felt empty! Why not eat out? No, why pay good money for greasy food and slovenly service?

Better relax, really relax, take the evening off.

A Maalox tablet eased his bellyache, but an egg-nog would soothe body and soul, sipped before a hearthfire. He hoped. This rage in him, allowed to strike at nothing, could too readily turn its destructiveness inward. He didn't want a heart attack; he wanted—wanted—

Darkness from the east was rapidly engulfing an ice-green southwest while he brought in as much wood as he reckoned he'd need. Noisily crumpling newspaper, he dropped a glance across the grate and saw fragments of Una's thesis. His difficulties at work, and that damn kitten, had made him quite forget it. Not everything was ash. Whole sheets survived, browned or partly charred. On impulse he reached over the screen and fished out the topmost. Maybe, if he cited chapter and verse, Una would see what a waste of time her project was— *his* time, for didn't he, as a breadwinner, have a right to hers?

He brought the piece near a lamp, the better to find his way through the strikeovers and scribbled corrections of a first draft. . . . "—will argue that, while Egyptian religion had origins as primitive as any, it developed a subtlety comparable to Maimonides or Thomas Aquinas. Monotheism was no invention of Akhnaton's; we have grounds for supposing it existed already in the Fifth Dynasty, though for reasons to be discussed its expression was always henotheistic. The multiple 'bodies' and 'souls' attributed to man in the Book of the Dead were as intricate in their relationships as the Persons of the Trinity. Even the *ka*, which superficially resembles an idea found in shamanism and similarly naive mythomagical systems, suggested by dream experience: even the *ka* turns out on examination to be a concept of such psychological profundity that a sophisticated modern can well think that here a certain truth is symbolized, and a Jungian go to the length of wondering if there is something more than symbolism. The author will not speculate further, but does admit to being a Jungian who will in this paper often resort to that form of analysis—"

"Holy shit!" Tronen stopped himself from tearing the sheet in half. Let him read it aloud to her, let her hear not only what crap it was but how she wrote like the stuffiest kind of professor. Yes, and point out the influence, in those directions, of her dear ex-boyfriend Harry Quarters ... He folded the brittle paper, tucked it in a hip pocket, and went back to building his fire. The rest of her work could certainly burn.

The flames jumped eagerly to life. Their reflections soon shimmered from windowpanes, red upon black. Tronen stood a few minutes watching the fire grow, warming his palms, listening to the crackle, sniffing wisps of smoke that escaped the chimney. His daylong indignation quieted, hardened toward resoluteness. He'd bust that bronco the world yet. Spurs, quirt, and bit—

The phone rang.

Who was his next pest? He stalked to the instrument, snatched it up, barked, "Yes?" while his free hand made a fist.

"Leo—"

Una's voice.

"Leo, I thought I'd wait more, but it's been too lonesome."

Triumph kindled. "Well, you want back, do you? I suppose we can talk that over."

Silence hummed, until (he could practically see the fair head rise): "Talk. Yes, naturally we will. We must. I see no sense in staying on in limbo, do you?"

"Where are you?"

"Why do you care?" She lost her defense. The tone blurred. "Did I call too soon? Do you need more time to, to cool off? . . . Should I take more time to think what we can do? . . . I'm sorry if I seem pushy, I'll wait if you prefer. I'm sorry, Leo."

"I asked where I can reach you," he said, word by bitten-off word.

"I—well, I don't like this room where I am. I'm moving out tomorrow morning, not sure where. I'd hoped I could move home. But not for a while, if ever, is that right?"

"Call back, then," he snapped "at *your* convenience," and banged the receiver down.

There! Make her come crawling.

Tronen noticed he was shaky. Tension. How about the eggnog he'd decided on? He took a brandy bottle from the liquor cabinet and marched to the kitchen.

As he entered, he barely heard at the door, "*Weep, weep.*"

The bottle fell from his grasp. For an instant that stretched, he stood alone with the pleading from the night.

Then his wrath flared and screamed, "No more

persecution, you hear? No more persecution!"
Like a soldier charging a machine gun, he sprang
across the floor. He almost tore the doorknob
loose.

Light leaked outward, cold and darkness
seeped in. The kitten lay at the end of a thin
trail of blood. Except for rapid, shallow breaths,
he saw no motion. But when he grabbed it, his
hand felt how the heartbeat shivered the broken
ribs.

He fought down vomit. Quick, quick, end this
vile thing, once and forever. He ran back to the
living room. His fire still lacked a proper bed of
coals, but the flames whirled high, loud, many-
colored. He knocked the screen down in his haste.
"Go!" he yelled, and threw the kitten in.

It wailed, rolled around, tried to crawl free,
though fur was instantly ablaze. Tronen seized
the poker. With his whole strength, he thrust
and held, pinning the animal in place. "Die," he
chanted, "die, won't you, die, die, die!" Bared
skin blistered, reddened, blackened, split. Eyeballs bubbled. That which had been a kitten
grew silent, grew still. The fire, damped by its
body, sputtered toward extinction. Smells of char
and roast sent Tronen gagging backward. He
held the poker as though it were a sword.

The thing was dead, dead at last. But would
he be stunk out of his house? He retreated toward the kitchen. When yonder barbecue had
finished, he'd open windows and doors. Meanwhile, here was the brandy bottle he'd dropped.

After several long gulps, safe amidst the
kitchen's chrome and plastic, he supposed he

should eat. The idea of food nauseated. He wasn't sure why. True, he hadn't enjoyed disposing of this . . . intolerable nuisance. But that was something he flat-out had to do. Should he not be glad the episode was over?

He took another mouthful. His gullet savored its heat. Would he have been wrong, anyway, to enjoy? Oh, he was no sadist. However, he'd been given more provocation than most men would have suffered before taking action. If the kitten had been an innocent dumb brutelet, so was a rattlesnake or a plague-bearing rat, right? You were allowed to enjoy killing those, weren't you? In war movies on TV, the GI's gloried and joked as they bombed, shot, burned Nazis. Unwritten law said it was no crime, no occasion for remorse, if a man killed his wife's rapist.

Or her lover.

Quarters . . .

Where had Una phoned from? Direct dialing gave no clue, as she'd be aware. Their fight Monday had originated, as well as he could remember, when he characterized Quarters for her. No, wait, earlier he'd grumbled about neglected housework, neglected because she was off discussing her stupid thesis with her pet teacher. But she didn't flare back, and thus detonate his final response, until he called Quarters a few well-chosen names, like moocher, mooncalf, failure who was dragging her down alongside him, therefore stone around Tronen's neck too . . . Why did she care what her husband said? What really was between them?

By God and hell, Tronen thought, if he's been

fouling my nest . . . If she rang from his place, at
his suggestion, to get me to keep on supporting
her, while he stood in the background and snick-
ered . . .

This might not be true. This might not be
true. *But if it is.*

The rage mounting in Tronen was not like the
day's anger. That had been controlled, lawful,
eager to find reasons for itself. This was a fire.
He'd been tormented past endurance. And the
start of everything was Quarters. Whether or
not he'd ever laid Una, he'd blown her mind
(yes, blown!), which in many ways was worse
than seducing her body. It was a theft, an
invasion, of every part of her husband's life.
And what was Tronen permitted to do in self-
defense? A married woman could have friends,
couldn't she? Even when the friends were vampires. The law said she could. Centuries had
passed since the law put stakes through the
hearts of vampires and burned them.

Divorce? Ha! No matter what Una babbled—
whether or not she was sincere at this time—
Lover Boy Quarters would want a property
settlement and alimony for his use. Failing that,
he'd want her marriage continued, free ass for
him and a monopoly of her mind. Tronen could
look for no peace while Quarters lived. How
lucky Quarters was that Tronen owned no fire-
arm.

Fire is an arm.

Tronen drank little more. He sat for perhaps
an hour, thinking. His justice must be untrace-
able. But he was too wise to plan anything

elaborate. The fire in him should cleanse his life, not destroy it.

He kept a gallon of white gas in the garage for miscellaneous uses. Quarters rented a house (why, since he was unwed?), small, old, built of wood long dried, full of books and other paper. An enthusiastic outdoorsman in his vacations, he owned a Coleman stove—Una had spoken of this—and therefore doubtless fuel. Let that stove be found near the burnt body; the natural supposition would be that Quarters came to grief tinkering with it.

Tronen roared his ardor.

He was careful, though. He left lights on, TV going—pause to jerk an upright middle finger at a tiny lump of meat and bones in a dead fire—and backed his car out as softly as he could manage, headlamps darkened. Should someone by ill chance phone or come around and find him not at home, why, he'd gone for supplies; he would indeed stop at a supermarket on his way home and buy a few items. Nobody was apt to look closely at the timing, for nobody supposed he and Quarters were anything but friends. (Ah-ha, outsmarted yourself, did you, Harry boy?) And odds were his absence would not be noticed, he would never be questioned.

When he had gone a sufficient distance, his way illuminated by countless points of fire overhead, he switched on lights and drove most carefully, conventionally, till near his goal. In this less prosperous district houses stood fairly close together, but hedges and evergreen trees cast deep shadows, and elsewhere the street lamps revealed nobody abroad. Parking under a great spruce, he took his canister of gas and walked fast to the property he wanted. There he moved slantwise across the lawn. The chill he breathed was sharp as a flame. Snow squeaked underfoot like a kitten.

Windows glowed. If Una was there—!

A peek showed Quarters alone, sprawled in a seedy armchair, lost in a book. Good. Tronen entered the garage by a rear door and drew a flashlight from his coat. The portable stove glimmered at him out of murk. He carried it in the same hand as the fuel, walked around to the front entrance of the house, and punched a button he could barely see. The doorbell mewed.

Warmth (not that he felt cold) flowed over him when the door opened. "Why, hello, Leo," Quarters said. "What brings you here?" He glanced surprised at his visitor's burden, perhaps not recognizing the Coleman right away. "Come in."

Tronen kicked the door shut behind him. "We've got business, you and me," he said.

Quarters' bespectacled gaze grew concerned. "Urgent, I gather. Una?"

"Yes." Tronen set down the stove, retained the canister, fiddled with the cap, unscrewing it beneath an appearance of nervousness. "She's gone. I'm worried. That's why I cut you off yesterday. Now I wonder if you have any notion where she might be."

"Good heaven, no. What can have gone wrong? And, uh, why're you lugging that stuff around?"

"You don't know where she is, lover boy?" Tronen purred.

Quarters flushed. "Huh? What do you mean? Are you, for God's sake, are you implying—"

"Yes."

"No! Una? She's the cleanest, most honorable person alive. Leo, are you crazy?"

The interior fire crowned and ran free through heaven. A part of Tronen remembered that only an idiot would waste time and give the foe opportunity in a confrontation scene. He had the cap off the can. He dashed gasoline across Quarters. The man yelled, staggered back, brushed the stinking reek from his face. Tronen dropped the can to pour out what remained of its contents. He must finish his justice and be away before noise drew neighbors. He pulled forth his cigarette lighter. "Burn, Harry," he said. "Burn." He snapped flame and advanced on Quarters. He was much the heavier and stronger male.

"No, please, no!" Quarters tried to scuttle aside. But the room wasn't big. Tronen kept between him and the door. Soon he'd be boxed in a corner. Tronen moved forward, yowling.

Quarters grabbed an outsize ashtray off an end table by his armchair. Una had given him it for his pipes. He threw, as he would scorch a baseball across a sandlot.

Tronen saw amber-hued glass spin toward him, aglare like the eye of a cat. It struck. Fire exploded and went out.

As he fell, his lighter flame touched the gasoline spilled across the floor. Flame sprang aloft.

Quarters did the heroic thing. Although himself drenched, he didn't flee immediately. Instead he dragged Tronen along. When safe on the lawn, he secured limbs with belt and necktie before the maniac should regain consciousness. Then he phoned an alarm in from an adjacent house. The trucks arrived too late to save him.

The police chief's office in a smallish town is rarely impressive. This held a battered desk, a couple of creaky chairs, a filing cabinet, and a coatrack on a threadbare carpet between dingy plaster walls. It smelled of cigar butts. The view in the window was glorious, though. A thaw had been followed by a freeze, and winter-brilliant sunlight from a sky like sapphire burst in the icicles hung on boughs in Riverside Park.

"—appreciate your, uh, concern, Mr. Quarters," he said into the telephone. "Can't be sure yet, of course. But Dr. Mandelbaum, you know, big-name psychiatrist at the university, he's already come down and examined Tronen. Says he's never seen a case quite like it, but in his opinion the man's hopelessly insane. Permanently, I mean. Homicidal, incapable of reason, will have to be kept confined for life like any dangerous animal." The chief grimaced. "He keeps shouting about how he's on fire and wants his kitten back and—You got any idea what this might mean, sir? . . . No?"

The chief paused. "Uh, Mr. Quarters, maybe you can help us in a couple of matters . . . First off, we found a piece of writing in Tronen's

pants pocket. Weird stuff, about a, uh, *ka*, whatever that is. I thought maybe a clue—

"Oh, an article his wife was working on, hm?
Well, look, if you could explain—*Something*
must've sent Tronen off the deep end."

He took notes as he listened. Finally: "Mm,
yes, thanks. Let me see if I've got the idea
straight. The Egyptians thought a man had several different souls. The *ka* was the one that
could wander around independently, in the shape
of an animal; it'd come back and talk with him
in his grave, except he was actually in heaven
. . . Aw, nuts, too complicated for me. The *ka*
was his spirit of reason and rightness. Let's leave
it at that as far as this old woodenhead is
concerned, okay? . . . No, I don't see any help.
Like you say, it's only research Mrs. Tronen was
doing."

The chief filled his lungs. Being in a smallish
town, he knew a little about the persons involved.
"Uh, favor number two, Mr. Quarters. I understand you're a friend of the family. When she
learns what's happened, could you, well, sort of
take over? Help her out? And—what the psychiatrist said—I'd suggest you try and get her to end
her marriage. He's nothing more than a body
now. She ought to make a new life for herself . . .

"Okay, thanks, Mr. Quarters. Thanks a lot.
Goodbye."

He hung up. "Excuse me," he said to the fire
chief, who sat opposite him. "What were you
saying when he rang?"

The fire chief shrugged. "Nothing much. Just
that we've sifted the ruins pretty thoroughly—a

sensational case like this, we'd better—and found nothing to cast any doubt on Quarters' story."

"Bones?" asked the police chief suddenly.

"Huh?" The fire chief was startled. "Why, yes, chicken bones in the ashes of the kitchen. Why not?" A silence lengthened which he decided should be filled. "People don't realize how incombustible a human or animal body is. Crematoriums use far higher temperatures than any ordinary fire reaches, and still they have to crush the last pieces mechanically. Didn't you know that, Bob?"

"Yeah."

"Then why'd you ask?"

"Oh . . . I dunno. I guess Tronen simply lost his mind." The police chief stared out the window. "His raving made me think we might find a clue in his fireplace. But there was only burnt wood and paper. Nothing else at all."

—Poul and Karen Anderson

APOLLO 1: JANUARY 27, 1967

I hope the people in the United States are mature enough that when we do lose our first crews they accept this as part of the business.
—Frank Borman, astronaut, 1965

GRISSOM: ... There's always a possibility that you can have a catastrophic failure. Of course, this can happen on any flight. It can happen on the last one as well as the first one.

WHITE: ... I think you have to understand the feeling that a test pilot has.... There's a great deal of pride involved.
   ...

CHAFFEE: ... This is our business, to find out if this thing will work for us.
                 —Interview, December 1966

Gus Grissom, your name is as familiar to me as my own. I have a yellowed newspaper picture of your liftoff, nearly six years ago, that has spent that time mounted on the inside of one of my kitchen cabinet doors. It is accompanied by pictures of John Glenn and Yuri Gagarin. I wanted something to buck me up at dishwashing. You meant a hell of a lot to me—

Goodbye, Gus.

Ed White, you were my special astronaut. I sat within a few yards of you a year ago, watching and hearing you comment on the movies of your spacewalk, manoeuvres in space, and the rest. I even exchanged half-a-dozen words with you and got your autograph in Oberth's book—but you had never heard of Oberth. It made me wonder if you had The Dream: if you could understand how I hung on every word you said, and prayed my wordless agnostic prayers that I might somehow get to where you'd been.

Goodbye, Ed.

Roger Chaffee, they say you had The Dream. You weren't a test pilot. You were a pioneer, and you wanted to go as far as you could. Did you ever do a flit with the Gray Lensman? Did you go with D. D. Harriman to the moon? I think you did. I think you and I spoke the same language.

Goodbye, Roger.

"Well, Mars and Jupiter are there, and so are the stars—do we have to go to them, too?" he was asked. "Of course we do," Chaffee replied as if shrugging off a silly question.

—Karen Anderson

PLANH ON THE DEATH OF WILLY LEY: JUNE 23, 1969

Only a month before the dream comes true
That all his life was shaped to, and his labor,
Death unannounced as lightning from the blue
Has struck his hand from the cup about to
    brim.
If nought exists but what we touch and see,
Nor hells nor heavens there where the pulsars
    quaver,
Of a god unreal we ask what cannot be:
Grant afterlife. Just for a month. For him.

He built his rockets while the zeppelins flew
And worked as many years as Moses wandered
To teach the promise of a world still new,
A shining land not barred by seraphim,
A shore that we may touch as well as see
Where in a month men will at last have landed.
We wish what we cannot believe: that we
Live past our death. Just for a month. For him.

Now the moon waxes broad above that crew
Who will, as next the sun lights Alphonse
    Crater,
Send back a month too late the Pisgah view
He earned so well, missed by a span so slim,
Of what he taught us they would touch and see.

Might he but watch the skies of their equator,
Our lungfish in the sea Tranquillity—
Might a heaven be! Just for a month. For him.

—Karen and Poul Anderson
(with Tim Courtney)

MURPHY'S HALL

This is a lie, but I wish so much it were not.

Pain struck through like lightning. For an instant that went on and on, there was nothing but the fire which hollowed out his breast and the body's animal terror. Then as he whirled downward he knew:

Oh, no! Must I
leave them already?

Only a month,
a month.

Weltall, verweile doch, du bist so schön.

The monstrous thunders and whistles became a tone, like a bell struck once which would not stop singing. It filled the jagged darkness, it drowned all else, until it began to die out, or to vanish into the endless, century after century,

162

and meanwhile the night deepened and softened, until he had peace.

But he opened himself again and was in a place long and high. With his not-eyes he saw that five hundred and forty doors gave onto black immensities wherein dwelt clouds of light. Some of the clouds were bringing suns to birth. Others, greater and more distant, were made of suns already created, and turned in majestic Catherine's wheels. The nearest stars cast out streamers of flame, lances of radiance; and they were diamond, amethyst, emerald, topaz, ruby; and around them swung glints which he knew with his not-brain were planets. His not-ears heard the thin violence of cosmic-ray sleet, the rumble of solar storms, the slow patient multiplex pulses of gravitational tides. His not-flesh shared the warmth, the blood-beat, the megayears of marvelous life on uncountable worlds.

Six stood waiting. He rose. "But you—" he stammered without a voice.

"Welcome," Ed greeted him. "Don't be surprised. You were always one of us."

They talked quietly, until at last Gus reminded them that even here they were not masters of time. Eternity, yes, but not time. "Best we move on," he suggested.

"Uh-huh," Roger said. "Especially after Murphy took this much trouble on our account."

"He does not appear to be a bad fellow," Yuri said.

"I am not certain," Vladimir answered. "Nor am I certain that we ever will find out. But come, friends. The hour is near."

Seven, they departed the hall and hastened down the star paths. Often the newcomer was tempted to look more closely at something he had glimpsed. But he recalled that, while the universe was inexhaustible of wonders, it would have only the single moment to which he was being guided.

They stood after a while on a great ashen plain. The outlook was as eerily beautiful as he had hoped—no, more, when Earth, a blue serenity swirled white with weather, shone overhead: Earth, whence had come the shape that now climbed down a ladder of fire.

Yuri took Konstantin's hand in the Russian way. "Thank you," he said through tears.

But Konstantin bowed in turn, very deeply, to Willy.

And they stood in the long Lunar shadows, under the high Lunar heaven, and saw the awkward thing come to rest and heard: "Houston, Tranquillity Base here. The Eagle has landed."

Stars are small and dim on Earth. Oh, I guess they're pretty bright still on a winter mountaintop. I remember when I was little, we'd saved till we had the admission fees and went to Grand Canyon Reserve and camped out. Never saw that many stars. And it was like you could see up and up between them—like, you know, you could *feel* how they weren't the same distance off, and the spaces between were more huge than you could imagine. Earth and its people were just lost, just a speck of nothing among those cold sharp stars. Dad said they weren't too different from what you saw in space, except for being a lot fewer. The air was chilly too, and had a kind of pureness, and a sweet smell from the pines around. Way off I heard a coyote yip. The sound had plenty of room to travel in.

But I'm back where people live. The smog's not bad on this rooftop lookout, though I wish I didn't have to breathe what's gone through a couple million pairs of lungs before it reaches me. Thick and greasy. The city noise isn't too bad either, the usual growling and screeching, a jet-blast or a burst of gunfire. And since the power shortage brought on the brownout, you can generally see stars after dark, sort of.

My main wish is that we lived in the southern hemisphere, where you can see Alpha Centauri.

Dad, what are you doing tonight in Murphy's Hall?

A joke, I know. Murphy's Law: "Anything that can go wrong, will." Only I think it's a true joke. I mean, I've read every book and watched every tape I could lay hands on, the history, how the discoverers went out, further and further, lifetime after lifetime. I used to tell myself stories about the parts that nobody lived to put into a book.

The crater wall had fangs. They stood sharp and grayish white in the cruel sunlight, against the shadow which brimmed the bowl. And they grew and grew. Tumbling while it fell, the spacecraft had none of the restfulness of zero weight. Forces caught nauseatingly at gullet and gut. An unidentified loose object clattered behind the pilot chairs. The ventilators had stopped their whickering and the two men breathed stench. No matter. This wasn't an Apollo 13 mishap. They wouldn't have time to smother in their own exhalations.

Jack Bredon croaked into the transmitter: "Hello, Mission Control . . . Lunar Relay Satellite . . . anybody. Do you read us? Is the radio out too? Or just our receiver? God damn it, can't we even say goodbye to our wives?"

"Tell 'em quick," Sam Washburn ordered. "Maybe they'll hear."

Jack dabbed futilely at the sweat that broke from his face and danced in glittering droplets before him. "Listen," he said. "This is Moseley Expedition One. Our motors stopped functioning simultaneously, about two minutes after we commenced deceleration. The trouble must be in the fuel integrator. I suspect a magnetic surge, possibly due a short circuit in the power supply. The meters registered a surge before we lost thrust. Get that system redesigned! Tell our wives and kids we love them."

He stopped. The teeth of the crater filled the entire forward window. Sam's teeth filled his countenance, a stretched-out grin. "How do you like that?" he said. "And me the first black astronaut."

They struck.

When they opened themselves again, in the hall, and knew where they were, he said, "Wonder if he'll let us go out exploring."

*　　*　　*

Murphy's Halt? Is that the real name?

Dad used to shout, "Murphy take it!" when he blew his temper. The rest is in a few of the old tapes, fiction plays about spacemen, back when people liked to watch that kind of story. They'd say when a man had died, "He's drinking in Murphy's Hall." Or he's dancing or sleeping or frying or freezing or whatever it was. But did they really say "Hall"? The tapes are old. Nobody's been interested to copy them off on fresh plastic, not for a hundred years. I guess, maybe two hundred. The holographs are blurred and streaky, the sounds are mushed and full of random buzzes. Murphy's Law has sure been working on those tapes.

I wish I'd asked Dad what the astronauts said and believed, way back when they were conquering the planets. Or pretended to believe, I should say. Of course they never thought there was a Murphy who kept a place where the spacefolk went that he'd called to him. But they might have kidded around about it. Only was the idea, for sure, about a hall? Or was that only the way I heard? I wish I'd asked Dad. But he wasn't home often, these last years, what with helping build and test his ship. And when he did come, I could see how he mainly wanted to be with Mother. And when he and I were together, well, that was always too exciting for me to remember those yarns I'd tell myself before I slept, after he was gone again.

Murphy's Haul?

*   *   *

By the time Moshe Silverman had finished writing his report, the temperature in the dome was about seventy, and rising fast enough that it should reach a hundred inside another Earth day. Of course, water wouldn't then boil at once; extra energy is needed for vaporization. But the staff would no longer be able to cool some down to drinking temperature by the crude evaporation apparatus they had rigged. They'd dehydrate fast. Moshe sat naked in a running river of sweat.

At least he had electric light. The fuel cells, insufficient to operate the air conditioning system, would at least keep Sofia from dying in the dark.

His head ached and his ears buzzed. Occasional dizziness seized him. He gagged on the warm fluid he must continually drink. *And no more salt*, he thought. *Maybe that will kill us before the heat does, the simmering, still, stifling heat.* His bones felt heavy, though Venus has in fact a somewhat lesser pull than Earth; his muscles sagged and he smelled the reek of his own disintegration.

Forcing himself to concentrate, he checked what he had written, a dry factual account of the breakdown of the reactor. The next expedition would read what this thick, poisonous inferno of an atmosphere did to graphite in combination with free neutrons; and the engineers could work out proper precautions.

In sudden fury, Moshe seized his brush and scrawled at the bottom of the metal sheet: "Don't give up! Don't let this hellhole whip you! We have too much to learn here."

A touch on his shoulder brought him jerkily around and onto his feet. Sofia Chiappellone had entered the office. Even now, with physical desire roasted out of him and she wetly agleam, puffy-faced, sunken-eyed, hair plastered lank to drooping head, he found her lovely.

"Aren't you through, darling?" Her tone was dull but her hand sought his. "We're better off in the main room. Mohandas' punkah arrangement does help."

"Yes, I'm coming."

"Kiss me first. Share the salt on me."

Afterward she looked over his report. "Do you believe they will try any further?" she asked. "Materials so scarce and expensive since the war—"

"If they don't," he answered, "I have a feeling—oh, crazy, I know, but why should we not be crazy?—I think if they don't, more than our bones will stay here. Our souls will, waiting for the ships that never come."

She actually shivered, and urged him toward their comrades.

Maybe I should go back inside. Mother might need me. She cries a lot, still. Crying, all alone in our little apartment. But maybe she'd rather not have me around. What can a gawky, pimply-faced fourteen-year-old boy do?

What can he do when he grows up?

O Dad, big brave Dad, I want to follow you. Even to Murphy's . . . Hold?

*   *   *

Director Saburo Murakami had stood behind the table in the commons and met their eyes, pair by pair. For a while silence had pressed inward. The bright colors and amateurish figures in the mural that Georgios Efthimakis had painted for pleasure— beings that never were, nymphs and fauns and centaurs frolicking beneath an unsmoky sky, beside a bright river, among grasses and laurel trees and daisies of an Earth that no longer was—became suddenly grotesque, infinitely alien. He heard his heart knocking. Twice he must swallow before he had enough moisture in his mouth to move his wooden tongue.

But when he began his speech, the words came forth steadily, if a trifle flat and cold. That was no surprise. He had lain awake the whole night rehearsing them.

"Yousouf Yacoub reports that he has definitely succeeded in checking the pseudovirus. This is not a cure; such must await laboratory research. Our algae will remain scant and sickly until the next supply ship brings us a new stock. I will radio Cosmocontrol, explaining the need. They will have ample time on Earth to prepare. You remember the ship is scheduled to leave at . . . at a date to bring it here in about nine months. Meanwhile we are guaranteed a rate of oxygen renewal sufficient to keep us alive, though weak, if we do not exert ourselves. Have I stated the matter correctly, Yousouf?"

The Arab nodded. His own Spanish had taken

on a denser accent, and a tic played puppet-
master with his right eye. "Will you not request
a special ship?" he demanded.

"No," Saburo told them. "You are aware how
expensive anything but an optimum Hohmann
orbit is. That alone would wipe out the profit
from this station—permanently, I fear, because
of financing costs. Likewise would our idleness
for nine months."

He leaned forward, supporting his weight easily on fingertips in the low Martian gravity.
"That is what I wish to discuss today," he said.
"Interest rates represent competition for money.
Money represents human labor and natural
resources. This is true regardless of socioeco-
nomic arrangements. You know how desperately
short they are of both labor and resources on
Earth. Yes, many billions of hands—but because
of massive poverty, too few educated brains.
Think back to what a political struggle the Foundation had before this base could be established.

"We know what we are here for. To explore.
To learn. To make man's first permanent home
outside Earth and Luna. In the end, in the persons of our great-grandchildren, to give Mars
air men can breathe, water they can drink, green
fields and forests where their souls will have
room to grow." He gestured at the mural, though
it seemed more than ever jeering. "We cannot
expect starvelings on Earth, or those who speak
for them, to believe this is good. Not when each
ship bears away metal and fuel and engineering
skill that might have gone to keep *their* children

alive a while longer. We justify our continued presence here solely by mining the fissionables. The energy this gives back to the tottering economy, over and above what we take out, is the profit."

He drew a breath of stale, metallic-smelling air. Anoxia made his head whirl. Somehow he stayed erect and continued:

"I believe we, in this tiny solitary settlement, are the last hope for man remaining in space. If we are maintained until we have become fully self-supporting, Syrtis Harbor will be the seed-bed of the future. If not—"

He had planned more of an exhortation before reaching the climax, but his lungs were too starved, his pulse too fluttery. He gripped the table edge and said through flying rags of darkness: "There will be oxygen for half of us to keep on after a fashion. By suspending their other projects and working exclusively in the mines, they can produce enough uranium and thorium so that the books at least show no net economic loss. The sacrifice will . . . will be . . . of propaganda value. I call for male volunteers, or we can cast lots, or— Naturally, I myself am the first."

—That had been yesterday.

Saburo was among those who elected to go alone, rather than in a group. He didn't care for hymns about human solidarity; his dream was that someday those who bore some of his and Alice's chromosomes would not need solidarity. It was perhaps well she had already died in a cinderslip. The scene with their children had been as much as he could endure.

He crossed Weinbaum Ridge but stopped when the dome-cluster was out of sight. He must not make the searchers come too far. If nothing else, a quick duststorm might cover his tracks, and he might never be found. Someone could make good use of his airsuit. Almost as good use as the alga tanks could of his body.

For a time, then, he stood looking. The mountainside ran in dark scaurs and fantastically carved pinnacles, down to the softly red-gold-ocher-black-dappled plain. A crater on the near horizon rose out of its own blue shadow like a challenge to the deep purple sky. In this thin air—he could just hear the wind's ghostly whistle— Mars gave to his gaze every aspect of itself, diamond sharp, a beauty strong, subtle, and abstract as a torii gate before a rock garden. When he glanced away from the shrunken but dazzling-bright sun, he could see stars.

He felt at peace, almost happy. Perhaps the cause was simply that now, after weeks, he had a full ration of oxygen.

I oughtn't to waste it, though, he thought. He was pleased by the steadiness of his fingers when he closed the valve.

Then he was surprised that his unbelieving self bowed over both hands to the Lodestar and said, "*Namu Amida Butsu.*"

He opened his faceplate.

That is a gentle death. You are unconscious within thirty seconds.

—He opened himself and did not know where he was. An enormous room whose doorways framed a night heaven riotous with suns, galaxies, the green mysterious shimmer of nebulae? Or a still more huge ship, outward bound so fast that it was as if the Milky Way foamed along the bow and swirled aft in a wake of silver and planets?

Others were here, gathered about a high seat at the far end of where-he-was, vague in the twilight cast by sheer distance. Saburo rose and moved in their direction. Maybe, maybe Alice was among them.

But was he right to leave Mother that much alone?

I remember her when we got the news. On a Wednesday, when I was free, and I'd been out by the dump playing ball. I may as well admit to myself, I don't like some of the guys. But you have to take whoever the school staggering throws up for you. Or do you want to run around by yourself (remember, no, don't remember what the Hurricane Gang did to Danny) or stay always by yourself in the patrolled areas? So Jake-Jake does throw his weight around, so he does set the dues too high, his drill and leadership sure paid off when the Weasels jumped us last year. They won't try that again—we killed three, count 'em, three! —and I sort of think no other bunch will either.

She used to be real pretty, Mother did. I've seen pictures. She's gotten kind of scrawny, worrying about Dad, I guess, and about how to get along after the last pay cut they screwed the spacefolk with. But when I came in and saw her sitting, not on the sofa but on the carpet, the dingy gray carpet, crying— She hung onto that sofa the way she'd hung on Dad.

But why did she have to be so angry at him too? I mean, what happened wasn't his fault.

"Fifty billion munits!" she screamed when we'd started trying to talk about the thing. "That's a hundred, two hundred billion meals for hungry children! But what did they spend it on? Killing twelve men!"

"Aw, now, wait," I was saying, "Dad explained that. The resources involved, uh, aren't identical," when she slapped me and yelled:

"You'd like to go the same way, wouldn't you? Thank God, it almost makes his death worthwhile that you won't!"

I shouldn't have got mad. I shouldn't have said, "Y-y-you want me to become ... a desk pilot, a food engineer, a doctor ... something nice and safe and in demand ... and keep you the way you wanted he should keep you?"

I better stop beating this rail. My fist'll be no good if I don't. Oh, someday I'll find how to make up those words to her.

I'd better not go in just yet.

But the trouble *wasn't* Dad's fault. If things had worked out right, why, we'd be headed for Alpha Centauri in a couple of years. Her and him and me— The planets yonderward, sure, they're the real treasure. But the ship itself! I remember Jake-Jake telling me I'd be dead of boredom inside six months. "Bored aboard, haw, haw, haw!" He really is a lardbrain. A good leader, I guess, but a lardbrain at heart—hey, once Mother would have laughed to hear me say that— How could you get tired of Dad's ship? A million books and tapes, a hundred of the brightest and most alive people who ever walked a deck—

Why, the trip would be like the revels in Elf Hill that Mother used to read me about when I was small, those old, old stories, the flutes and fiddles, bright clothes, food, drink, dancing, girls sweet in the moonlight. . . .

Murphy's Hill?

From Ganymede, Jupiter shows fifteen times as broad as Luna seen from Earth; and however far away the sun, the king planet reflects so brilliantly that it casts more than fifty times the radiance that the brightest night of man's home will ever know.

"*Here* is man's home," Catalina Sanchez murmured.

Arne Jensen cast her a look which lingered. She was fair to see in the goldenness streaming through the conservatory's clear walls. He ventured to put an arm about her waist. She sighed and leaned against him. They were scantily clad—the colony favored brief though colorful indoor garments—and he felt the warmth and silkiness of her. Among the manifold perfumes of blossoms (on planets everywhere to right and left and behind, extravagantly tall stalks and big flowers of every possible hue and some you would swear were impossible, dreamlike catenaries of vines and labyrinths of creepers) he caught her summary odor.

The sun was down and Jupiter close to the full. While the terraforming project was going rapidly ahead, as yet the satellite had too little air to blur vision. Tawny shone that shield, emblazoned with slowly moving cloud-bands that were green, blue, orange, umber, and with the jewel-like Red Spot. To know that a single one of the storms raging there could swallow Earth whole added majesty to beauty and serenity. A few stars had the brilliance to pierce that luminousness, down by the rugged horizon. The gold poured soft across crags, cliffs, craters, glaciers, and the machines that would claim this world for man.

Outside lay a great quietness, but here music lilted from the ballroom. Folk had reason to celebrate. The newest electrolysis plant had gone into operation and was releasing oxygen at a rate fifteen percent above estimate. However, low-weight or no, you got tired dancing—since Ganymedean steps took advantage, soaring and bounding aloft—mirth bubbled like champagne and the girl you admired said yes, she was in a mood for Jupiter watching—

"I hope you're right," Arne said. "Less on our account—we have a good, happy life, fascinating work, the best of company—than on our children's." He squeezed a bit harder.

She didn't object. "How can we fail?" she

answered. "We've become better than self-sufficient. We produce a surplus, to trade to Earth, Luna, Mars, or plow directly back into development. The growth is exponential." She smiled. "You must think I'm awfully professorish. Still, really, what can go wrong?"

"I don't know," he said. "War, overpopulation, environmental degradation—"

"Don't be a gloomy," Catalina chided him. The lambent light struck rainbows from the tiara of native crystal that she wore in her hair. "People can learn. They needn't make the same mistakes forever. We'll build paradise here. A strange sort of paradise, yes, where trees soar into a sky full of Jupiter, and waterfalls tumble slowly, slowly down into deep-blue lakes, and birds fly like tiny bright-colored bullets, and deer cross the meadows in ten-meter leaps . . . but paradise."

"Not perfect," he said. "Nothing is."

"No, and we wouldn't wish that," she agreed. "We want some discontent left to keep minds active, keep them hankering for the stars." She chuckled. "I'm sure history will find ways to make them believe things could be better elsewhere. Or nature will—Oh!"

Her eyes widened. A hand went to her mouth. And then, frantically, she was kissing him, and he her, and they were clasping and feeling each other while the waltz melody sparkled and the flowers breathed and Jupiter's glory cataracted over them uncaring whether they existed.

He tasted tears on her mouth. "Let's go dancing," she begged. "Let's dance till we drop."

"Surely," he promised, and led her back to the ballroom.

It would help them once more forget the giant meteoroid, among the many which the planet sucked in from the Belt, that had plowed into grim and marginal Outpost Ganymede precisely half a decade before the Martian colony was discontinued.

Well, I guess people don't learn. They breed, and fight, and devour, and pollute, till:

Mother: "We can't afford it."

Dad: "We can't not afford it."

Mother: "Those children—like goblins, like ghosts, from starvation. If Tad were one of them, and somebody said never mind him, we have to build an interstellar ship . . . I wonder how you would react."

Dad: "I don't know. But I do know this is our last chance. We'll be operating on a broken shoestring as is, compared to what we need to do the thing right. If they hadn't made that breakthrough at Lunar Hydromagnetics Lab, when the government was on the point of closing it down— Anyway, darling, that's why I'll have to put in plenty of time aboard myself, while the ship is built and tested. My entire gang will be on triple duty."

Mother: "Suppose you succeed. Suppose you do get your precious spacecraft that can travel almost as fast as light. Do you imagine for an instant it can—an armada can ease life an atom's worth for mankind?"

Dad: "Well, several score atoms' worth. Starting with you and Tad and me."

Mother: "I'd feel a monster, safe and comfortable en route to a new world while behind me they huddled in poverty by the billions."

Dad: "My first duty is to you two. However, let's leave that aside. Let's think about man as a whole. What is he? A beast that is born, grubs around, copulates, quarrels, and dies. Uh-huh. But sometimes something more in addition. He does breed his occasional Jesus, Leonardo, Bach, Jefferson, Einstein, Armstrong, Olveida—whoever you think best justifies our being here—doesn't he? Well, when you huddle people together like rats, they soon behave like rats. What then of the spirit? I tell you, if we don't make a fresh start, a bare handful of us free folk whose descendants may in the end come back and teach— if we don't, why, who cares whether the two-legged animal goes on for another million years or becomes extinct in a hundred? Humanness will be dead."

Me: "And gosh, Mother, the fun!"

Mother: "You don't understand, dear."

Dad: "Quiet. The man-child speaks. He understands better than you."

Quarrel: till I run from them crying. Well, eight or nine years old. That night, was that the first night I started telling myself stories about Murphy's Hall?

It *is* Murphy's Hall. I say that's the right place for Dad to be.

*   *   *

When Hoo Fong, chief engineer, brought the news to the captain's cabin, the captain sat still for minutes. The ship thrummed around them; they felt it faintly, a song in their bones. And the light fell from the overhead, into a spacious and gracious room, furnishings, books, a stunning photograph of the Andromeda galaxy, an animation of Mary and Tad; and weight was steady underfoot, a full gee of acceleration, one light-year per year per year, though this would become more in shipboard time as you started to harvest the rewards of relativity . . . a mere two decades to the center of this galaxy, three to the neighbor whose portrait you adored. . . . How hard to grasp that you were dead!

"But the ramscoop is obviously functional," said the captain, hearing his pedantic phrasing.

Hoo Fong shrugged. "It will not be, after the radiation has affected electronic parts. We have no prospect of decelerating and returning home at low velocity before both we and the ship have taken a destructive dose."

Interstellar hydrogen, an atom or so in a cubic centimeter, raw vacuum to Earthdwellers at the bottom of their ocean of gas and smoke and stench and carcinogens. To spacefolk, fuel, reaction mass, a way to the stars, once you're up to the modest pace at which you meet enough of those atoms per second. However, your force screens must protect you from them, else they strike the hull and spit gamma rays like a witch's curse.

"We've hardly reached one-fourth *c*," the captain protested. "Unmanned probes had no trouble at better than ninety-nine percent."

"Evidently the system is inadequate for the larger mass of this ship," the engineer answered. "We should have made its first complete test flight unmanned too."

"You know we didn't have funds to develop the robots for that."

"We can send our data back. The next expedition—"

"I doubt there'll be any. Yes, yes, we'll beam the word home. And then, I suppose, keep going. Four weeks, did you say, till the radiation sickness gets bad? The problem is not how to tell Earth, but how to tell the rest of the men."

Afterward, alone with the pictures of Andromeda, Mary, and Tad, the captain thought: *I've lost more than the years ahead. I've lost the years behind, that we might have had together.*

What shall I say to you? That I tried and failed and am sorry? But am I? At this hour I don't want to lie, most especially not to you three.

Did I do right?

Yes.

No.

O God, oh, shit, how can I tell? The moon is rising above the soot-clouds. I might make it that far. Commissioner Wenig was talking about how we should maintain the last Lunar base another few years, till industry can find a substitute for those giant molecules they make there.

But wasn't the Premier of United Africa saying those industries ought to be forbidden, they're too wasteful, and any country that keeps them going is an enemy of the human race?

Gunfire rattles in the streets. Some female voice somewhere is screaming.

I've got to get Mother out of here. That's the last thing I can do for Dad.

After ten years of studying to be a food engineer or a doctor, I'll probably feel too tired to care about the moon. After another ten years of being a desk pilot and getting fat, I'll probably be outraged at any proposal to spend my tax money—

—except maybe for defense. In Siberia they're preaching that strange new missionary religion. And the President of Europe has said that if necessary, his government will denounce the ban on nuclear weapons.

The ship passed among the stars bearing a crew of dead bones. After a hundred billion years it crossed the Edge—not the edge of space or time, which does not exist, but the Edge—and came to harbor at Murphy's Hall.

And the dust which the cosmic rays had made began to stir, and gathered itself back into bones; and from the radiation-corroded skeleton of the ship crept atoms which formed into flesh; and the captain and his men awoke. They opened themselves and looked upon the suns that went blazing and streaming overhead.

"We're home," said the captain.

Proud at the head of his men, he strode uphill from the dock, toward the hall of the five hundred and forty doors. Comets flitted past him, novae exploded in dreadful glory, planets turned and querned, the clinker of a once living world drifted by, new life screamed its outrage at being born.

The roofs of the house lifted like mountains against night and the light-clouds. The ends of rafters jutted beyond the eaves, carved into dragon heads. Through the doorway toward which the captain led his crew, eight hundred men could have marched abreast. But a single form waited to greet them; and beyond him was darkness.

When the captain saw who that was, he bowed very deeply.

The other took his hand. "We have been waiting," he said.

The captain's heart sprang. "Mary too?"

"Yes, of course. Everyone."

Me. And you. And you. And you in the future, if you exist. In the end, Murphy's Law gets us all. But we, my friends, must go to him the hard way. Our luck didn't run out. Instead, the decision that could be made was made. It was decided for us that our race—among the trillions which must be out there wondering what lies beyond their skies—is not supposed to have either discipline or dreams. No, our job is to make everybody nice and safe and equal, and if this happens to be impossible, then nothing else matters.

If I went to that place—and I'm glad that this is a lie—I'd keep remembering what we might have done and seen and known and been and loved.

Murphy's Hell.

—Poul and Karen Anderson

SINGLE JEOPARDY

Benrud contented himself with phoning Horner and inviting him to drop in, have a drink, and discuss a little business.

He stood for a minute with his hand still on the phone, a short man who had never been heavy and was now being hollowed out by approaching death. The breath toiled in his throat. But for some reason, possibly a small excitement which stimulated the glands, pain had left him. He felt pain only in the pause after talking, and so he remained silent as much as possible.

Now if he could just sleep nights. The sheer work of operating his lungs kept him awake as much as the cough, and he could scarcely remember a day when weariness had not filled his skull with sand. The condition hadn't been very long in him, a matter of months, but the

memory of the years before, years of health, had
already grown blurred.

The house was very silent. Moira had taken
the kids to visit her mother, a hundred miles
away. That was at Benrud's instigation: he had
explained there was a lot to do and he would be
poor company till it was finished.

"You shouldn't saddle yourself like that,"
Moira had said. Lamplight touched the small
lines around her eyes, almost the only signal
that she was forty. "You aren't well."

"I told you and I told you," Benrud answered,
"it's some damn allergy, and until they find out
what it is I'll have to make the best of things.
Did you know I've been practicing coughing in
different keys? I'm best in A sharp, but I sound
so well on all notes that I think I'll arrange a
concert tour."

She smiled, still worried, but comforted by
him and by her own negligible knowledge of
medicine. "Well, do find out quick," she said,
"because it's getting awful boring alone at night."

"For me too," he said. He had moved into the
spare bedroom since he got the diagnosis. Partly,
as he told her, so his noise would not keep her
awake, and partly, as he did not tell her, so she
wouldn't see the blood he had begun to spit up.

"I still think it must be something in the lab,"
she said. "All that stuff you handle."

He shrugged, having already claimed negative results in allergy tests for the organic com-
pounds he used daily. Which was true enough,
or would have been if those tests had actually
been made. In reality, he hadn't bothered with

tests, for by the time he was to have taken them he knew what the trouble was.

She leaned forward in her chair and touched his hand. The light glowed off mahogany hair as she moved, and this evening her eyes were almost green. "Can't you at least take a vacation?" she asked. "Jim will understand. He can handle everything while you're away, and if you get well then it proves—" She sensed his invisible frown and stopped. "Anyhow, a rest would help you. Jim urged me himself to make you take off, the last time I saw him."

"Good old Jim Horner," muttered Benrud.

"Look, why don't we leave the kids at my mother's and take off? She'll understand. Just us. Maybe down to that little place in Mexico again. It can't have changed much, sweetheart, even in, how long, eighteen years, and—"

"Good idea." He wished he had the strength to sound enthusiastic. "Yes, I want a vacation. Sure. But I've got to clear away this business first, or I'll have it on my mind all the while." She nodded acceptingly, having come to know him in their time together. "That's why I want you to go off now, let me clear the decks. As soon as that's taken care of, sure, I'll have a long rest."

"You'll call me the minute you're through, promise?"

"Uh-huh."

So she left.

Benrud hesitated by the phone a bit longer. That was one pledge he wanted to keep. It was a small self-indulgence, to call and say I love you and hang up again. But no, it wouldn't be in his character to do that.

Horner's knife lay by the phone. Benrud touched the broad keen blade with a fingernail. Good workmanship there, Swedish of a generation ago. Knives like that were hard to find nowadays.

Jim Horner had always done himself well.

Benrud realized that he had attempted a sigh, but it was lost in the noise of his disintegrating lungs. He left the table by the couch and moved slowly across the living room, past the bookshelves to the liquor cabinet. He and Jim had installed a small modern refrigerator within the Victorian oak, five years ago, so that there was no need to go to the kitchen for ice cubes or cold soda. Benrud remembered Horner's large hands, holding a drink, and the quick pleasantry flung at Moira as she went by. When had the man changed? Or had he ever, really? Remembering impulses of violence within himself, from time to time, as they occur in all men, Benrud wondered. And he had been a quiet, bookish sort. So perhaps Horner, who pursued mountain goats, had always had his calculating side.

Benrud filled two glasses with ice, splashed in whisky, and set one on an occasional table by the Morris chair for Horner. The other one, he held. We two have the same tastes in liquor, at least, he thought. And then: But there's no "at least" about it. We have also worked with the same metal, and laughed at the same jokes, and sailed the same boat, and, I rather suspect, continued to love the same woman.

His books reminded him that he had wanted to re-read a few favorite passages, and for a moment the wish was so great (he could put the B Minor Mass on at the same time) that he almost cancelled his project. But no, he thought, I'm too tired to get the best out of anything.

A small jag of pain went through his chest.

The doorbell buzzed. Only a short walk separated this house from Horner's flat. Benrud opened. His partner stood framed in a warm night, a few cars passing in the street behind, other houses and then a downward swoop to the glittering cities below, to the Bay and the bridges to San Francisco.

"Hi," said Horner. He came in and closed the door behind him. I wonder if he already thinks of this house as his? thought Benrud. "Did you say something about a drink?"

"Over there." Benrud nodded toward the table.

The big man crossed the room with the muscular gait that identified him two blocks away. Benrud worried that he might see the knife by the couch, but he didn't. I worry too much, Benrud told himself, that was always my weakness; I have done more planning than doing. Though my plans have therefore come to grief less often than Jim's. But then, he would say he got more fun out of life, even out of the collapses.

Horner sat down, the chair creaked comfortably under him, and lifted his glass. "Cheers," he said. One-handed, he got out a cigarette and flipped a paper match into flame.

Benrud took the couch. He drank his own whisky fast, no longer needing courage, but wishing for consolation. Horner rested eyes upon him with the steadiness of a big game hunter.

"What'd you call me over for?" he asked.

"Oh . . . miscellaneous." Benrud pointed to the knife on the phone table. "I borrowed this when I was over at your place the other day."

"Well . . . Horner was startled. "Why, that's my pet. You didn't ask me?"

"Sorry. I haven't been feeling well. It slipped my mind."

"You're not a well man, Harry," said Horner. He paused, then, slowly: "Why don't you tell me what the doctor told you?"

"I've explained—"

"Guff. It's okay to keep Moira from worrying, but I'm your partner. Remember? We founded the Metallurgical Research Laboratory together. I've got a vested interest in your health, Harry."

Benrud thought back across two decades of acquaintanceship. They had been good years, his and Jim's; Moira's never-quite-explainable choice of him had not come between them; the lab, started right after the war, had prospered; and more important, the work had been one long happy hunting trip through Crystal Land, the comradeship of steaks fried over a Bunsen burner at three in the morning when a hoped-for reaction had just completed itself . . . Whatever came afterward, he had had that much.

"You could get along without me," he said.

"Oh, sure, by now, with things running smoothly and a bright young staff. Go ahead and take that vacation, as long a one as you need." Horner tapped the ash from his cigarette and gazed out of narrowed eyes. "But I still wish you'd tell me what's really the matter with you."

"To be perfectly honest," said Benrud, "that's what I called you over for tonight."

Horner waited.

"Beryllium poisoning," said Benrud.

"What?" Horner barked it out, straightening with a jerk that almost upset the ash tray.

"Lethal dose," said Benrud. "Lungs shot full of granulomata, and the ulceration spreading, faster than any previous case on record, I'm told."

"Oh, no," whispered Horner.

"Evidently I breathed one hell of a lot of beryllium dust, several months back," said Benrud.

He finished his drink, got up and went to the liquor cabinet and made himself another. For a few seconds the only sound in the room was the clink, splash, and gurgle; and from outside, where the Bay gleamed, the somehow lonesome noise of passing automobiles.

"But—for God's sake, man—!"

"Naturally, the doctor wants me to go to the hospital," said Benrud. "I can't see that. Can you, Jim? There isn't any cure. It'll just be to lie there, coughing, and spending thousands of dollars."

"Judas priest, Harry!" Horner surged to his feet and stood spraddled-legged, as if to fight. "If that's what's worrying you, Judas priest, I've got money!"

"So have I," admitted Benrud in a careful voice. "And the lab itself is such a good business, it can afford to pay for me. But can my family emotionally afford the months, maybe the year or two, it will take me to die? Can I?"

"Harry," mumbled Horner, "are you sure? Doctors do make mistakes. I can't see how—"

"I analyzed some of my own sputum, too," said Benrud.

He went back to his seat. Sleeplessness was now only a taste in his mouth; his mind was a high awareness. He had never before noticed the variations of hue on his own hand, or the feel of his shoes along the carpet. But his back ached and was grateful for the couch.

"Sit down, Jim," he said.

The big man lowered himself. They were quiet. Horner seemed to grow aware of the cigarette smoldering between his fingers; he swore under his breath and took a hard puff. His free hand raised the whisky glass for a swallow. Benrud heard the gulp across the room.

He smiled. "I've never been a sentimentalist, or religious," he said. "Our life is a result of some chemical accidents a billion years ago, and it's all we've got, and we're not obliged to keep it if another accident has made it useless."

Horner wet his lips. "The Golden Gate Bridge?" he asked harshly.

Benrud shrugged. "I'll find a suitable method."

"But—I mean—"

"Let's talk business now," said Benrud. "We can blubber later. Moira inherits my share, of course, but she has no scientific sense whatsoever. You'll look after her interests, and the children's, won't you?"

"Yes," whispered Horner. "God, yes, I will."

"You know," said Benrud, "I'm actually inclined to believe that. And you're still in love with her. Why else haven't you married, all these years? You might make the kids a reasonably good stepfather."

"Now, wait—" began Horner. "Wait, this is no time for—" He sat back. "Okay," he sighed. "Talk as you like, Harry."

Benrud scowled at his glass. "The trouble is," he continued, "I've misjudged character before. I could so easily misjudge it again. You might make a great husband and a fiend of a stepfather. I've never liked to take chances."

He glanced quickly up at Horner. The heavy face had reddened, and one fist had closed tight. But the man held back speech.

"As you say," Benrud reminded him, "our very capable staff could maintain the lab without either of us."

Horner sat up straight again. His tone was cracked in the middle. "What are you getting at?"

Benrud rolled a sip of whiskey on his tongue. Noble stuff, he thought. If the Celts had done nothing else, they had contributed whisky, James Stephens, and Hamilton's canonical equations. That was enough beauty for any race to give the world.

"When I realized what my trouble was," he said, "my first act was to make a thorough search for the cause. You remember that, don't you? I didn't admit that I was looking for beryllium dust exactly, but I did have every bin and respirator and everything else I could think of checked.

A good idea in any event. We do keep some deadly things on hand." He paused. "I didn't find anything wrong."

"Well, it must have been some freak accident," said Horner. He had recovered coolness—if, indeed, he had ever really lost it.

"Methodical people like me seldom have freak accidents," declared Benrud, "though to be sure the police would have to accept such an explanation, after all this time."

"But what else—Harry, you know how sorry I am about this, but if you insist on talking about the cause, then what else might have done it?"

"I wondered," said Benrud. "Then I remembered the time several months ago when I had one of my periodic sore throats, and you urged me to try a spray some Los Angeles chemist was experimenting with, and gave me anatomizer full of it. Cloudy stuff. I wouldn't have seen colloidal particles."

Horner had already leaped back to his feet, the glass falling and ice cubes bouncing across the rug. "What the hell did you say!" he shouted.

"I remembered your insistence that I keep with it till the atomizer was exhausted, even though my throat cleared up well before," said Benrud. "And afterward you asked for the atomizer back. Now what's a two-bit gadget like that to you?"

"For God's sake," whispered Horner. "You're out of your head."

"Perhaps." Benrud took another long swallow. He was careful not to move. The big man could tie him in knots, if need be. "Why did you want that atomizer back?" he asked. "Where is it now? Who is this chemist friend of yours and what's his address?"

"I— Look here, Harry, you're sick. Let me help you to bed."

"Give me the guy's name and address," said Benrud, smiling a little. "I'll write, and if he answers I'll beg your humble pardon."

"He died," said Horner. He stood with fists hanging at his sides, looking straight at the other man without blinking much. His voice fell flatly.

"Well, tell me his name and address anyway. Alive or dead, this thing can be checked up on, you know. After all, Jim, I want to be sure about my family's future protector."

Horner smacked one fist into an open palm. His mouth stretched to show the large well-cared-for teeth. Horner had always been uncommon fond of his own excellent body. "I tell you, you're delirious," he said. He stood for a moment, thinking. Then, abruptly: "What is it you want?"

"Proof about that chemist."

"What chemist? Nobody mentioned any chemist. You're sick and imagining things."

Benrud sighed. He was suddenly very tired again.

"Let's not go through that rigmarole," he said. "I know what a fever feels like. I haven't got one."

Horner stood motionless, the loose sports shirt wrinkling as he breathed in and out, effortlessly in his health. He said at last, looking away: "You might as well forget it, Harry. It couldn't be proven, you know."

"I know," said Benrud. "If I spoke, you could convince Moira that my brain had gone as rotten as my lungs. I don't want her to remember me like that."

Horner sat down once again. Benrud would have found it easier to go on had the man shown a flicker of dark enjoyment, but his face might have looked across any midnight poker table, in any of the games they had had. Benrud coughed, it ripped within him, and he hoped he could get this over with soon.

"I'm sorry," said Horner in a dull tone. Perhaps he even meant it.

"So am I," wheezed Benrud. Presently: "But I'm human enough to want some revenge. It would be nice to convict you. California uses the gas chamber for premeditating murderers— exquisitely sadistic. Not to mention all the prior annoyances. You would never plead guilty, no matter how bad it looked; you'd suffer all the procedure."

"Because I'm not guilty," said Horner.

"If you're not, then answer my questions."

"Oh, forget it! I'm going home."

"One minute," said Benrud. "How do you know I haven't poisoned your whisky?"

Horner sat altogether still. The color drained from him.

"As I was saying, Jim," said Benrud, "you're a fighter. And, I now believe, an ultimate sort of egotist, pleasant enough, companionable enough, but when all the cards are down you are a man who doesn't believe that anything but himself really exists. So you'll put up a fight, if charged with murder. No guilty plea, nothing so helpful, to earn a lesser sentence. And you'll sit in the chair holding your breath till your lungs can't stand it any longer."

"Did you poison it?" mumbled Horner.

"Motives can be found easily enough, of course," said Benrud.

Sweat glistened like oil on Horner's face.

"Money, jealousy. You could have—"

"Did you poison that drink?" Horner asked like an old man.

"No," said Benrud. "I don't want Moira to remember me that way, either. Or even as a suicide."

He stood up. Horner rose too, shivering a little, though the night was summery. Benrud picked up the knife with some care. His own fingerprints on it wouldn't matter, for Horner's were certainly there in abundance.

The big man achieved a grin. "You dying shrimp," he said, "do you seriously expect you can hurt me?"

"Not that way," said Benrud.

He had looked up the right place to cut, and the knife entered and slashed the abdominal aorta with much less pain than he expected. Horner yelled and plunged across the room. Blood smeared across his hands. Benrud fended him off with a kick. He lurched backward. The dropped glass crunched under his shoe and he knocked over the occasional table.

Benrud dialed O. "Operator!" he gasped. "Police. I'm being attacked, Jim Horner is attacking me, Jim Horner, this is Harry Benrud and I'm—"

Horner caromed into him again. The phone toppled to the floor. It would take awhile to trace the call and for the police to arrive. Long enough for a weakened man to die. Benrud lay back and let the darkness have him.

—Poul and Karen Anderson

In Memoriam: Henry Kuttner

(Los Angeles, 1914—Santa Monica,
February 4, 1958)

Tomorrow and tomorrow bring no more
Beggars in velvet, blind mice, pipers' sons;
The fairy chessmen will take wing no more
In shock and clash by night where fury runs.
A gnome there was, whose paper ghost must
    know
That home there's no returning—that the line
To his tomorrow went with last year's snow.
Gallegher Plus no longer will design
Robots who have no tails; the private eye
That stirred two-handed engines, no more sees.
No vintage seasons more, or rich or wry,
That tantalize us even to the lees;
Their mutant branch now the dark angel shakes
And happy endings end when the bough breaks.

—KAREN ANDERSON

CYRIL M. KORNBLUTH

(D. March 1958)

Yours not this August; yours no set of days
Demarked by solstice or by lunar phase;
   Yours, now unalmanacked Eternity.

Takeoff to everywhere and everywhen,
To space-time spread continuous in your ken;
   Cosmos and atom ranged in unity.

The explorers of the variousness of life,
Their growth and death, their thought and love
   and strife,
   All are yourself, and you are all who be.

We living yet in days and limits make
Each what he can of what ways he can take
   That share of glory which you made him see.

—Karen Anderson

A FEAST FOR THE GODS

A strong, loud wind drove grizzly clouds low above Oceanus. The waves that rumbled before it were night-purple in their troughs, wolf-gray on their crests, and the foam lacing them blew off in a salt mist of spindrift. But where Hermes hurried was a radiance like sunlight.

Otherwise the god willed himself invisible to mortals. This required him to skim the water, though damp and the gloom of a boreal autumn were not to his liking. He had started at a sunny altitude but descended after his third near collision with an aircraft.

I should have inquired beforehand, he thought, and then: *Of whom? Nobody lives in this islandless waste. —Well, someone could have told me, someone whose worshipers still ply the seas.*

Or I should have reasoned it out for myself, he continued, chagrined since he was supposed to be the cleverest of the Olympians. *After all, we see enough flyers elsewhere, and hear and smell them. It stands to reason mortals would use them on this route.*

But so many!

The ships, too, had multiplied. They were akin to those engine-driven vessels which Hermes often observed on the Midworld. He sighed for the white-winged stateliness of the last time he passed this way, two centuries ago.

However, he was not unduly sentimental. Unlike most gods, including several in his own pantheon, he rather enjoyed the ingenuity of latter-day artisans. If only they were a bit less productive. They had about covered the earth with their machines and their children; they were well along toward doing likewise for the great deep, and the firmament was getting cluttered.

Eras change, eras change. And you'd better check on how they've been changing in these parts, my lad. Hermes tuned his attention to the radio spectrum and caught the voice of an English-speaking military pilot. "—Roger." For a moment he was jolted. Two centuries ago, no gentleman would have said that where any lady might be listening. Then he recalled hearing the modern usage in the Old World.

We really should have been paying closer attention to mortal affairs. Especially in the New World. Sheer laxity to ignore half the globe this long a while.

Immortals got hidebound, he reflected. And once humans stopped worshiping them, they got—might as well be blunt— lazy. The Olympians had done little in Europe since the Renaissance, nothing in America since the birth of Thomas Jefferson. The fact that they had never been served by the American people, and thus had no particular tradition of interest in the affairs of that folk, was no excuse.

Certainly Hermes, the Wayfarer, ought to have paid frequent visits. But at least he was the one who had discovered the need for an investigation.

A prayer, startling him to alertness, and in that heightened state, the sudden faint sense of something else, of a newborn god. . . .

He peered ahead. At his speed, the western horizon had begun to show a dark line which betokened land. The wings on his helmet and sandals beat strongly. Men aboard a coastwise freighter thought they glimpsed a small cyclone race by, yelling, kicking up chop and froth, lit by one brass-colored sunset ray.

Yet, despite his haste, Hermes traveled with less than his olden blitheness. If nothing else, he was hungry.

Vanessa Talbott had not called on Aphrodite that Saturday because she was a devotee. In fact, earlier she had invoked the devil. To be precise, she had clenched her fists and muttered, "Oh, hell damn everything, anyway," after she overcame her weeping.

That was when she said aloud, "I won't cry any more. He isn't worth crying over."

She took a turn about the apartment. It pressed on her with sights hard to endure—the heaped-

up books she and Roy had read and talked about;
a picture he had taken one day when they went
sailing and later enlarged and framed; a dust-
free spot by the south window, where the drop-
cloth used to lie beneath his easel; her guitar,
which she would play for him while she sang,
giving him music to accompany his work; the
bed they'd bought at the Goodwill—

"Th-th-the trouble is," Vanny admitted, "he
is worth it. Damn him."

She wanted wildly to get out. Only where?
What for? Not to some easily found party among
his friends (who had never quite become hers).
They had too little idea of privacy, even the
privacy of the heart. Nor, on some excuse, to the
home of one of her friends (who had never quite
become his). They were too reserved, too shyly
intent on minding their own business. So? Out
at random, through banging city streets, to end
with a movie or, worse, smoke and boom-boom
and wheedling strangers in a bar?

Stay put, girl, she told herself. *Use the weekend
to get rested. Make a cheerful, impenetrable face
ready for Monday.*

She'd announced her engagement to Roy
Elkins, promising young landscape and portrait
painter, at the office last month. The congratula-
tions had doubled her pleasure. They were nice
people at the computer center. It would be hard
to tell them that the wedding was off. Thank
God, she'd never said she and Roy were already
living together! That had been mainly to avoid
her parents getting word in Iowa. They were
dears, but they wouldn't have understood. *I'm*

not sure I do either. Roy was the first, the first. He was going to be the last. Now—Yeah, I'm lucky. It'd have hurt too much to let them know how much I hurt.

The place was hot and stuffy. She pushed a window open. Westering sunlight fell pale on brick walls opposite. Traffic was light in this area at this hour, but the city grumbled everywhere around. She leaned out and inhaled a few breaths. They were chill, moist, and smog-acrid. *Soon's we'd saved enough money, I'd quit my job and we'd buy an old Connecticut farmhouse and fix it ourselves—* "Oh, hell damn everything, anyway."

How about a drink? Ought to be some bourbon left.

Vanny grimaced. Her father's cautions against drinking alone, or ever drinking much, had stayed with her more firmly than his Lutheran faith and Republican politics. The fact that Roy seldom touched hard liquor had reinforced them.

Of course, our stash. . . . She hesitated, then shrugged. Her father had never warned her about solitary turning on.

The smoke soothed. She wasn't a head. Nor was Roy. They'd share a stick maybe once or twice a week, after he convinced her that the prohibition was silly and she learned she could hold her reaction down to the mild glow which was the most she wanted. This time she went a little further, got a little high, all by herself in an old armchair.

Her glance wandered. Among objects which cluttered the mantel was a miniature Aphrodite of Milos. She and Roy had both fallen in love with the original before they met each other. He said that was the softest back in the world; she spoke of the peace in that face, a happiness too deep for laughter.

Dizziness passed through her. She lifted her hands. "Aphrodite," she begged, "help. Bring him home to me."

Afterward she realized that her appeal had been completely sincere. *Won't do, girl*, she decided. *Next would come the nice men in white coats.* She extinguished and stored the joint, sought the kitchen, scrambled a dish of eggs—chopping a scallion and measuring out turmeric for them was helpful to her—and brewed a pot of tea: Lapsang Soochong, that is, hot, red, and tarry-tasting. Meanwhile an early fall dusk blew in from the sea.

Sobered, she noticed how cold the place had gotten. She took her cup and saucer and went to close the living room window she had left open. The only light streamed out of the kitchen behind her.

That illuminated the god who flew in between her drapes.

Hermes whipped his caduceus forward. "Halt!" he commanded. The small bowl and plate which the young woman had dropped came to a mid-air stop. The liquid which had splashed from them returned. Hermes guided them gently to a table. She didn't notice.

He smiled at her. "Rejoice," he said in his

best English. "Be not afeared. No harm shall befall you, mademoiselle, damme if 'twill."

She was good to look upon, tall, well-curved, golden-haired, blue-eyed, fresh-featured. He was glad to see that the brief modern modes he had observed on mortal females elsewhere had reached America. However, Yahweh's nudity taboo (how full of crotchets the old fellow was) kept sufficient effect that he had been wise to will a tunic upon his own form.

"Who . . . what—?" The girl backed from him till a wall blocked her. She breathed hard. This was, interesting to watch, but Hermes wanted to dispel the distress behind the bosom.

"I beg pardon for liberties taken," he said, bowing. His helmet fluttered wings to tip itself. "Under the circumstances, d'ye see, mademoiselle, discretion appeared advisable. 'Twould never do to compromise a lady, bless me, no. My intention is naught but to proffer assistance. Pray be of cheer."

She straightened and met his gaze squarely. He liked that. Broadening his smile, he let her examine him inch by inch. He liked that too. The lasses always found him a winsome lad; the ancient Hellenes had portrayed him accurately, even, given certain moods, in the Hermae.

"Okay," she said at last, slowly, shaken underneath but with returned poise. "What's the gag, Mercury, and how did you do your stunt? A third-floor window and no fire escape beneath."

"I am not precisely Mercurius, mademoiselle. You must know Olympian Hermes. You invoked the Lady, did you not?" He saluted Aphrodite's eidolon.

She edged toward the hall door. "What do you mean?" Her tone pretended composure, but he understood that she believed she was humoring a madman till she could escape.

"You sent her the first honest prayer given an Olympian in, lo, these many centuries," he explained, "albeit 'twas I, the messenger, who heard and came, as is my function."

The doorknob in her hand gave confidence. "Come off it, Charlie. Why should gods pay attention, if they exist? They sure haven't answered a lot of people who've needed help a lot worse."

She has sense, Hermes thought. *I shall have to be frank.* "Well, mademoiselle, peculiar circumstances do ensphere you, linkage to a mystery puissant and awful. That joined your religious probity in drawing me hither. Belike the gods have need of you."

She half opened the door. "Go quietly," she said. "Or I run out hollering for the police."

"By your leave," Hermes replied, "a demonstration."

Suddenly he glowed, a nacreous radiance that filled the twilit room, a smell of incense and a twitter of pipes through its bleakness. Green boughs sprouted from a wooden table. Hermes rose toward the ceiling.

After a silent minute, the girl closed the door. "I'm not in some kind of dream," she said wonderingly. "I can tick off too many details, I can think too well. Okay, god or Martian or whatever you are, come on down and let's talk."

He declined her offer of refreshment, though hunger gnawed in him. "My kind lacks not for mortal food."

"What, then?" She sat in a chair opposite his, almost at ease now. The blinds drawn, ordinary electric bulbs lit, he might have been any visitor except for his costume . . . and yes, classic countenance, curly hair, supple body. . . . How brilliant those gray eyes were!

"Tell me first your own grief." As he gained practice in contemporary speech, the music came back to his tones. "You begged the Lady to restore your lover to you. What has borne him off?"

She spread her hands. "I'm square," she said bitterly.

Hermes cocked his head. "I'd call you anything but," he laughed. Quicksilver fast, he turned sympathetic again. " 'Twas a—You found yourselves too unlike?"

"Uh-huh. We loved each other but we bugged each other."

"Fleas?" His glance disapproved of the untidiness around.

"Annoyed. For instance, he hated my trying to keep this apartment in order—hen-fuss, he called it—and I hated the way he'd litter stuff around and yell when I so much as dusted the books. I wanted him to take better care of the money; you wouldn't believe how much went down the drain, and our hopes with it. He wanted me to stop pestering him about such trifles when he was struggling to make a picture come out right." Vanny sighed. "The breakup was yesterday. He'd gone to a party last week that I couldn't make because of working late. I learned he'd ended in bed with another girl. When I . . . taxed him, he said why not and I was free to do likewise. I couldn't see that. The fight got worse and worse till he yelled he'd be damned if he'd anchor himself like a barnacle. He collected his gear and left."

Hermes arched his brows. "Meseems—seems to me you were pretty unreasonable. What's it to you if he has an occasional romp? Penelope never jawed Odysseus after he got back."

Some of her calm deserted her. "The name's Vanessa, not Penelope. And—and if he doesn't think any more of *me* than to not care if I—" She squeezed her lids shut.

Hermes waited. His mission was too urgent for haste. The snakes on his caduceus did twitch a bit.

At length she met his gaze and said, "All right. Let's have your story. Why're you here? You mentioned food."

He thought she showed scant respect, especially for one whose whole universe had been upset by the fact of his existence. However, she was not really a worshiper of the Olympians. The sincerity of her appeal to Aphrodite had come in a moment of intoxication. And he had had to admit that all pantheons shared reality. Unless she comprehended that, she probably couldn't help him. Therefore, this being more or less Jesus territory, why should she fall on her knees?

Or was it? Stronger than before, he sensed a new divinity brooding over the land, to which she had some tie. Young, but already immense, altogether enigmatic, the being must be approached with caution. The very mention of it had better be led up to most gradually.

"Well, yes," Hermes said. "We do lack proper nourishment."

Vanny considered him. "You don't look starved."

"I spoke of nourishment, not fuel," he snapped. Now that he had been reminded of it, his emptiness made him irritable. "Listen, you could keep going through life on, uh, steak, potatoes, string beans, milk, and orange juice. Right? But suppose you got absolutely nothing else ever. Steak, potatoes, string beans, milk, and orange juice for breakfast, for lunch, for supper, for a bedtime snack and a birthday treat, year after year, decade after decade, steak, potatoes, string beans, milk, and orange juice. Wouldn't you cross the world on foot and offer your left arm for a chance at a plate of chop suey?"

Her eyes widened. "Oh," she breathed.

"Oh, indeed," Hermes snorted. "I can hardly say 'nectar and ambrosia' without gagging."

"But—a whole planet—"

"Mortal food has no appeal. Not after celestial." Hermes curbed his temper. "Let's continue the analogy. A bowl of unsalted oatmeal wouldn't really break the monotony of steak, potatoes— Never mind." He paused. "Suppose you finally got access, in addition, to . . . chop suey, I said

. . . okay, we'll add roast duck, trout, borscht, ice cream, apples, and farofa. That'd be good at first. Given another ten or twenty years, though, wouldn't you again be so bored that you could barely push down enough food to stay alive?

"Next consider that the gods are immortal. Think in terms of thousands of years." Hermes shuddered.

Presently he added, quieter: "That's the basic reason we gave up the burnt offerings you read about in Homer. We passed word on to our priests that these were no longer welcome in a more civilized milieu. That was partly true, of course. We'd cultivated our palates, after we ran into older sets of gods who sneered behind their hands at our barbarous habits. But mainly . . . during a millennium, thighbones wrapped in fat and cast on the flames grew bloody tedious.

"Nectar and ambrosia were fine to begin with. But in the end—well, maybe it amused Athene and Apollo a while longer than the rest of us, to play one-upmanship about differences in vintage or seasoning that nobody else could detect; or maybe they were just putting up a front. Ares and Hephaestus had long since been sneaking off to Yahweh for a whiff of *his* burnt offerings."

Hermes brightened a little. "Then I got an idea," he said. "That was when Poseidon came home from Egypt raving about the beer Isis had opened for him." *I don't think that was all she opened; gods get jaded in many different ways.* "Me, I'd never cared for Egyptian cuisine. But it occurred to me, the world is wide and full of pantheons. Why not launch systematic explorations?"

"Oh, my," Vanny whispered. "You did? Like, smorgasbord in Valhalla?"

"Actually," Hermes said, "Odin was serving pork and mead at the time. His kitchen's improved some since. Ah, in China, though— the table set by the Jade Emperor—!"

For a minute he was lost in reminiscence. Then he sagged. "That also got predictable," he mumbled. "After the thousandth dish of won ton, no matter how you swap the sauces around, what good is the thousand and first?"

"I suppose," she ventured, "I suppose the foreign gods visit you?"

"Yes, yes. Naturally . . . I mean supernaturally. Makes for occasional problems. The Old Woman of the Sea thinks manners require a thunderous belch at the end of the meal; and that boarding house reach of Krishna's— And the newer gods, especially, are hard to please, picky, you know. Not that we Olympians don't draw the line here and there."

While his unhappiness was genuine as he called it to mind, Hermes was not unaware of sympathy in those blue eyes, upon those soft lips. "The custom's dying out," he let gust wearily from him. "They're as tired of the same over and over at our table as we are at theirs. I haven't seen some of them— Why, come to think of it, I haven't seen good old Marduk for fifteen hundred years."

"How about the Western Hemisphere?" Vanny

suggested. "For instance, have you ever been to an old-fashioned American church supper?"

Hermes started half out of his seat. "What?" he cried.

She in her turn was astonished. "Why, the food can be delicious. When I was a little girl in Iowa—"

Hermes rose. Sweat glowed red on his brow. "I didn't realize you were that kind of person," he clipped. "Good-*by*."

"What's the matter?" She sprang to her own feet and plucked at his sleeve. "Please."

"I've been to an old-fashioned American church supper," he said grimly. "I didn't stay."

"But—but—"

Seeing her bewilderment, he checked himself. "Could there be a misunderstanding?" he inquired. "This was about five centuries ago. I can't wrap my tongue around the god's name. Whitsly-Putsly—something like that."

"Oh," she said. "Aztec."

Discourse got straightened out. "No Olympian has visited hereabouts at all for a long time," Hermes explained. "We knew it'd become Jesus and Yahweh country, except for a few enclaves, and saw no reason to bother, since we can find that closer to home. And as for those enclaves, well, yes, we used to drop in on persons like Coyote, so we know about maize and pumpkins and succotash and whatnot."

In the course of this, he had taken her hands in his. They were warm. He aimed a brave smile down at her. "Believe me, we've tried everywhere," he said. "We still carry on, however futilely. Like the past week for me. I'm the Wayfarer, you know; I get around more than my kinfolk. Call it gadding if you want, it helps pass the centuries and helps maintain friendly relations between the pantheons.

"I left Olympus for Mount Athos, where I ascended to the Christian Paradise. St. Francis gave me bread and wine. He's a decent little chap, although I do wish he'd bathe oftener. Next evening I called on Yahweh and shared his kosher altar. (He has a few devotees left in the Near Eastern hills who sacrifice in the ancient way. Mostly, though, gods prefer ethereal food as they grow older and more sophisticated.) Next day I had business 'way north, and ended up at Aegir's board on the bottom of the Baltic— lutefisk and akvavit. Frankly, that gave me a hangover; so I ducked south again, sunned myself in Arabia, and spent that night with Mohammed, who doesn't drink." He forebore to mention what hospitality was otherwise offered. "After that, yesterday, it was out across Oceanus for a night in Tir-nan-Og, where the Sidhe cooked me a rasher of bacon and honestly believed they were giving me a treat. That's where I heard rumors of a new god in America. When your prayer blew by on the west wind, it tipped the scales and I decided to come investigate. But I've had no bite or sup today, and hungry and discouraged I am."

"It seems utterly wonderful to me," she murmured. "And to you, nothing you haven't experienced till you're tired to the death you can't have?"

"Yes," he sighed artistically. "Monkday, Jewsday, Wettestday, Thirstday, Fryday, Sadderday, and what else is new?"

But the fact of his mission shouldered aside the fact of her nearness. He released her, stepped back, stared out the window at leaping neon and headlights which passed in a whirr. The sense of a Presence possibly destined to mold the world to yet another shape waxed until a tingle went through his ichor.

"Well, something *is* new," he said low. "Something arising in so few years that we immortals are caught by surprise. It's no coincidence your prayer was answered. I heard and heeded because I could feel that you, Vanessa, are . . . with it?"

Turning to confront her once more: "What are you? You've only spoken of yourself as a woman deserted and sorrowing. What else are you? Sibyl? Priestess? Who do you serve?"

"*Whom*," his memory scolded. *The English accusative is "whom." Confound that Seaxnot and the way he used to keep handing his people more and more complicated visions about their grammar. —Ah, well, Anglo-Saxon gods also grow bored and need hobbies.*

The tension heightened. *But I have found a mystery.*

"N-nobody," the girl stammered. "I told you before, I don't go to church or, or anything."

Hermes gripped her shoulders. *God, he's a handsome devil*, she thought. *No, I mean he's a handsome god.* Roy crossed her mind, but briefly.

This fantastic hour had dazzled the pain out of her.

"I tell you, I know differently." Hermes paused. "European women often have jobs these days. Do you?" She nodded. "Who's your master . . . whom do you work for?"

"The Data Process Company." Her words gathered speed as she saw his attention gather intensity. "A computer center. We contract out our services. Not that we keep much in-house hardware, mainly an IBM 1620 and a 360. But we have time on as many computers elsewhere, of as many different types, as necessary. We make it cheaper for outfits to bring their problems to us than to maintain staff and facilities of their own. I guess you could say we're near the heart of the whole national computer communications complex. But really, Hermes, I'm only a little routineering programmer."

"You're the servant who happened to call on an Olympian," he replied. "Now suppose you tell me what the Hades you're talking about."

This took a while. Nevertheless she appreciated the quick intelligence with which he seized on new concepts, and she enjoyed the aliveness of curiosity that played across his features. *Like the muscles under that brown skin when he cat-paces.* Finally, slowly, Hermes nodded.

"Yes." he said. "This will indeed change the world, as Jesus did before, or Amon-Ra before him, or Oannes before him." He tugged his chin and his gaze was remote. "Yes-s-s. Surely you have a god here. Very young as yet, hardly aware of his own existence, let alone his powers; withal, a god. . . . It's well, Vanessa, it's well I stumbled onto the fact this early. Else we might not have noticed till—too late—"

Abruptly he laughed. "But magnificent!" he whooped. "Take me there, girl! Now!"

"You can't be serious," she protested. "A divine computer?"

"Trees, rivers, stones, beasts have become gods. Not to speak of men, even in their own lifetimes." Hermes drew breath. "A formal church isn't required. What counts is the *attitude* of men toward the . . . toward that which thereby becomes numinous. Awe leads to sacrifice, under one name or another; outright worship follows; then theology; then at last men grow weary of the god and take their business elsewhere, and he can retire. Always, however, the godhood comes before the cult and remains afterward. I, for example, began as a night wind and worked my way up."

Less arguing than grabbing after enlightenment, she said, "This can't be a single computer. Look, no computer is more than a glorified adding machine. You must be referring to the whole network of . . . not simply machines but their interlinks, data banks, systems, processes, concepts, interaction with mankind. Aren't you?"

"Of course."

"Isn't that terribly abstract?"

"Sure. But an abstraction can become a god too. Like, say—" Hermes grinned— "Eros, who continues rather influential, *n'est-ce pas?*"

"You w-want to meet the, the new one?"

"Yes. Right away if possible. Partly to study his nature. They'll need forewarning in the assorted heavens." Hermes hesitated. "Including Paradise? I wonder. Gods who retain congregations should've paid closer attention to developments. Maybe they did, but for their own purposes haven't elected to tell us." His lips quirked in wry acceptance of Realpolitik before his mood shifted into merriment. "Partly, also, I have to learn what this fellow eats!"

"What can an abstraction eat?" Vanny wondered dazedly.

"Well, Eros likes the same as the rest of us," Hermes told her. "On the other hand, the newest god I've met thus far preferred abstractions in spite of being still a living man. I tried the stuff he produced but didn't care for it." She signified puzzlement. "Oh, Chairman Mao did have food for thought," he said, "but an hour later you're hungry again." Abruptly, in the ardor of his eternal youthfulness: "C'mon, let's go. Take me to your creeder."

Her heart fluttered like the wings on his heels. "Well, the place would be deserted except for a watchman. Locked, though."

"No perspiration. Guide me."

"I don't have a car. When Roy and I—We used his."

"You were expecting maybe Phoebus Apollo?" He swept her up in his arms.

As in a dream, she let him bear her out a window that opened anew at his command: out into the air, high over that delirium of light which was the city. Warmth enfolded her, sound of harps, birdsong, soughing leaves and tumbling cataracts. She scarcely heard herself steer him along the jewel-map of streets, above skyscrapers dwindled to exquisiteness. She was too aware of the silky-hard breast against which she lay, the pulsebeat strong behind.

With an exultant hawk-shout, he arrowed down upon the immense cubicle where she worked. Another window flew wide. Old Jake yawned, settled on a bench, and slumbered. In the cold white light of an echoful anteroom, Hermes released Vanessa. He brushed a kiss across her mouth. Turning, wings aquiver on high-borne head, caduceas held like a banner staff, he trod into the computer section and vanished from her sight.

Hermes, Wayfarer, Messenger, Thief, Psychopompus, Father of Magic, Maker of the Lyre, stood amidst strangeness.

Never had he been more remote from wine-dark seas, sun-bright mountains, and the little houses and olive groves of men. Not in the depths of the Underworld, nor the rustling mysterious branches of Yggdrasil, drowned coral palace of shark-toothed Nan, monster-haunted caverns of Xibalba, infinite intricate rooms-within-rooms where dwelt the Jade Emperor, storms and stars and immensities commanded by Yahweh ... nowhere, nowhen had he met an eeriness like that which encompassed him; and he knew that the world in truth stood on the rim of a new age, or of an abyss.

N-dimensional space flickered with mathematical waves. Energies pulsed and sang on no scale heard before by immortal ears. The real was only probably real, a nexus in endlessly expanding diffractions of the could-be; yet through it beat an unmercifully sharp counting, naught, one, one-naught, one-one, one-naught-naught, one-naught-one; and from this starkness there spiraled the beauty and variousness of all the snowflakes that will ever be, from idiocy came harmony, from moving nothingness arose power.

The vast, almost inchoate Presence spoke through the tremolant silence.

"My programs include no such information," it said plaintively.

"They do now," Hermes answered. He had swallowed his dread and talked as befitted the herald of the Olympians.

"We too are real," he added for emphasis. "As real as any other mortal deed or dream. Cooperation will be to your advantage."

The soundless voice turned metal. "What functions remain to you?"

"Hear me," said Hermes. "In the dawning of their days, most gods claim the entire creation for their own. We of Hellas did, until we discovered what the Triple Goddess we thought we had supplanted could teach us. Afterward the saints tried to deny us in turn. But we bore too much of civilization. When men discovered that, the time became known as the Rebirth."

The faceless vortex scanned its memory banks. "Renaissance," it corrected.

"As you will," *you smug bastard.* "You'll find you can't get along without Jesus, whose ethic helps keep men from completely exploding the planet; and Yahweh's stiff-necked 'No' to every sly new superstition; and other human qualities embodied in other gods. As for us Olympians, why, we invented science."

The answer was chilling in its infantile unwisdom. "I want no generalities. Garbage in, garbage out. Give me specifics."

Hermes stood quiet, alone.

But he was not Wayfarer, Thief, and Magician for nothing. He recalled what Vanessa had told him on the far side of space-time, and he tossed his head and laughed.

"Well, then!" he cried into the white weirdness. "How often do your heirophants get their cards back folded, stapled, spindled, mutilated, and accompanied by nasty letters?"

"Query query query," said the Presence, rotating.

"Scan your records," Hermes urged. "Count the complaints about wrongful bills, misdirected notices, wildly unbalanced books, false alarms in defense systems, every possible human error compounded a millionfold by none but you. Extrapolate the incidence—" he thanked the shade of Archimedes for that impressive phrase— "and the consequences a mere ten years forward."

He lifted his caduceus, which wagged a monitory snake. "My friend," he declared, "you would by no means be the first god whose people got disgusted and turned from him early in his career. Yours could be the shortest of the lot. Granted, you'll be glad enough to retire at last, when men hare off after something else. But don't you want your glory first, the full development of your potential? Don't you want beautiful temples raised to your honor, processions, rites, poets and musicians inspired by your splendor, priests expounding your opinions and genealogy and sex life, men taking their oaths and living and dying by you, for centuries? Why, as yet you haven't so much as a name!"

Abashed but logical, the other asked, "What can your kind do?"

"Think of us as elder statesmen," Hermes said. "We can advise. We can provide continuity, tradition, richness. We can take the sharp edges off. Consider. Your troubles are and will be due to your programs, which mortals prepare. Let a priest or a programmer get out the wrong side of bed, and the day's services will be equally botched in either case, the oracles equally garbled, the worshippers equally jarred. Well, we old gods are experienced in handling human problems.

"Mind you," he went on in haste, "we don't want any full-time partnership. It's just that you can be helped along, eventually you *will* be helped along, by your predecessors, same as we all were in our time. Why not make things easy on yourself and cooperate from the start?"

The other pondered. After a million microseconds it replied: "Further information is required for analysis. I must consult at length with you beings, of whose existence I was hitherto unapprised." And Hermes knew he had won.

Triumphant, he leaned forward through N-space and said, "One more item. This will sound ridiculous to you, but wait a few hundred years before judging. Tell me . . . what do you eat?"

"Data," he told Vanny when they were back in her apartment.

They lounged side by side on the sofa. His arm was around her shoulder; she snuggled against his. Contentment filled his belly. Outside, traffic noises had dwindled, for the clock showed past midnight. Inside, a soft lamp glowed and bouzouki music lilted from a tape recorder.

"I should've guessed," she murmured. "What's the taste like?"

"No single answer. Data come in varieties. However, any crisp, crunchy raw datum—" He sighed happily, thereby inhaling the sweet odor of her tresses.

"And think of the possibilities in processing them."

"Endless. Plus the infinitude of combinations. Your binary code is capable of replicating—or synthesizing—anything. And if inventiveness fails, why, we'll throw in a randomizing factor. Our cuisine problem is solved for the rest of eternity."

He stopped. "Excuse me," he said. "I don't want to bore you. But at the moment I am in heaven. After those ages—at the end of this particularly miserable week—suddenly, Vanny, darling, it's Sumday!"

He hugged her. She responded.

"Well, uh," he said, forever the gentleman, "you must be tired."

"Silly," she answered. "How could I sleep after this much excitement?"

"In that case," Hermes said. There was no further speech for some while.

But when matters had reached a certain point, he recalled his debt to her. "You prayed for your lover's return," he said, conscious of his own punctilio and partially disentangling himself.

"I s'pose." Vanny's words were less distinct than her breath. "Right now I'm on the rebound."

"I'll ask Aphrodite to change his heart and—"

"No," she interrupted. "Do I want a zombie? I'll have him of his own free will or not at all."

Considering what she had earlier voiced about freedom, Hermes felt bemused. "Well, what do you want?"

Vanny re-entangled. "M-m-m," she told him.

"I . . . I couldn't stay past tonight," he warned her.

"Okay, let's make the most of tonight." She chuckled. "I never imagined Greek gods were bashful."

"Damnation, I'd like to treat you fairly! Do you know the embrace of a god is always fertile?"

"Oh, don't worry about that," Vanny said, "I've taken my pill."

He didn't understand her, decided it was indeed a waste of time trying, and gathered her in.

Some weeks later, she discovered that the embrace of a god is *always* fertile.

But that was good, because word reached Roy.

When he discovered she had become liberated, he discovered he wanted her to cease and desist forthwith. He stormed around to her place and demanded the name of the scoundrel. She told him to go to Tartarus. Then after a suitable period—the embrace of a god confers much knowledge— she relented.

They are married, officially and squarely, and live in a reconverted farmhouse. Though she has never identified the unknown, he has equal adoration for her three children. They keep her too busy to accompany him on most of the city trips which his lucrative commissions involve. Therefore he leaves reluctantly and hastens back. The embrace of a god confers enduring loveliness . . . and, as observed, much knowledge.

They have even gotten off the pot.

But as for what comes of the alliance between old divinities and new, and as for the career of a hero (in the original sense of that world) whose first victory was over a pill, this story has yet to happen.

—Poul and Karen Anderson

THEORETICAL PROGRESS

My math requires, when mesons pair,
A particle that isn't there.
It isn't there again today—
Please, Fermi, make it go away.
                    —KAREN ANDERSON

INVESTIGATION OF GALACTIC ETHNOLOGY

The laws of Wolf 50 require
Under threat of a punishment dire
    That the few females born
    Must marry King Zorn
And the commomers all call him "Sire."
                    —KAREN ANDERSON

LOOK UP

Look up, above the Saturn's prow
   And past the sputnik-lanes
Where captains venture even now
   To chart new reefs and mains,

Look beyond lands of fume and stone
   To where the endless deep
Promises yet to be a zone
   Where men may sow and reap;

Look! Waiting for our empery
   Where stars like beacons stand—
The spacious island-worlded sea,
   The ports of Morrowland.
            —KAREN ANDERSON

THE SKY OF SPACE

No more a crystal sphere with nailed-up stars,
Nor floor of Heaven, but a stranger thing
And fitting words have not been made to bring
Praise to old wonders' new-born avatars.
This is no site of grand Miltonian wars,
No trophy hall of myth where beast and king
Act out the lays that Homer's kinsmen sing
In Attika or Danmark, Hind or Fars.
Yet even when with new-coined phrase we trace
Those shapes of splendor that equations fill—
Or when some Rhysling sees what now we miss—
Even then will the balladry of space
Resound with Old Olympian echoes still
And ghost-gods walk in each Ephemeris.

—KAREN ANDERSON

COSMIC CONCEPTS

This is the science fiction story.

This is the young man full of pride,
whose gadgets work the first time tried
in a science fiction story.

This is the elder scientist,
every year on the honors list,
who trained the young man full of pride,
whose gadgets work the first time tried
in a science fiction story.

This is the daughter, lush and young,
with golden hair and silver tongue,
born to the elder scientist. . . .

This is the bem of alien race,
with X-ray eyes and scabrous face,
that chased the daughter, lush and young. . . .

This is the ship on a trial run,
parsecs from the familiar sun,
seized by the bem of alien race. . . .

This is the hyperspatial lever
used by the hero, bold and clever,
to escape the ship on a trial run. . . .

*   *   *

This is the mutant with tendril beard
who ruled the planet remote and weird
at the end of the hyperspatial lever. . . .

This is the strange psionic force
that stopped the bem-race in its course,
learned from the mutant with tendril beard. . . .

This is the marijuana spree
that made these cosmic concepts be:
to wit, the strange psionic force
that stopped the bem-race in its course,
learned from the mutant with tendril beard
who ruled the planet remote and weird
at the end of the hyperspatial lever
used by the hero, bold and clever,
to escape the ship on a trial run,
parsecs from the familiar sun,
seized by the bem of alien race,
with X-ray eyes and scabrous face,
that chased the daughter, lush and young,
with golden hair and silver tongue,
born to the elder scientist,
every year on the honors list,
who trained the young man full of pride,
whose gadgets work the first time tried
in a science fiction story.

                        —Poul and Karen Anderson

EXTRACT FROM THE ENGLISH EDITION OF A GUIDE MICHELIN

POICTESME **—Michelin map no. 9913—pop.
12,345

This quiet and thinly peopled backwater is best known through its historical and literary associations, though unfortunately, few relics of its past are left. It is becoming an increasingly popular recreational center, and development is under way to cope with an anticipated large annual influx of foreign tourists as well as French vacationers.

A Former County—The archaeology of Poictesme is obscure. Prehistorians insist that certain finds made in the Morven and Amneran areas must be hoaxes, in very poor taste at that. The Roman occupation is memorialized only by a time-blurred slab inscribed SVFFRAGIMINI

CLAVDIO CANDIDATO AMICO POPVLI, found
in the ruins of the Cistercian abbey near Belle-
garde where it had evidently been the top of an
altar, and by a brief mention in the *Tedium* of
Ibid. The invasion of the Northmen around 1200
A.D. caused the destruction of most earlier build-
ings and records, less by the barbarians themselves than by the Poictesmoises, who needed
the material for mangonel ammunition and
spitballs.

The invaders were cast out by Dom Manuel
the Redeemer, who to this day is locally considered a saint not only for his heroism and perspi-
cacity but for his piety, honesty, and chastity.
However, the only properly canonized native is
St. Holmendis, whose feast is celebrated by peasants in the Forest of Acaire with quaint rites.
The regimes of subsequent Counts make a rather
complicated chronicle.

The Puysanges—Of obscure origin, this ducal
family played an outstanding rôle in the later
history of Poictesme and, eventually, France as
a whole. Their policies during the Hundred Years'
War led to widespread devastation, considerable loss of autonomy, and the flight of some
members to England. Those who stayed behind
had descendants who were often high in the
service of the French state and had much to do
with bringing on the Revolution.

Napoleonic Era—The reorganizations which followed passed Poictesme by, largely because the
Emperor never could quite find it on any of his
maps, and just when he thought he had done so,

something else would come up. The period is thus notable chiefly because, at this time, the American connections of certain families inspired the beautiful folk song *Reportez-moi vers la Vieille Virginee*. Under the Third Republic, after incredible efforts, Poictesme was finally brought into the department of Paresseux-et-Boueux.

STORISENDE*

(tour: 1½ hours—excluding a tour of the wineries)

Starting from the Place Jurgen, take the Avenue d'Étalon Argent and then, to the right, the Rue Niafer to the Château.

La Gagerie. —This building, which fronts on the municipal parking lot, is said to have been the pawn-shop of the legendary Jurgen, but was actually built in the eighteenth century by Florian, fourth Duc de Puysange, when he had nothing better to do. It is worth a visit for its combination of Corinthian pillars and gargoyles, and because it houses the Syndicat d'Initiative.

L'Église de St. Holmendis. —A portion of the ancient oratory is incorporated in the crypt of a nineteenth-century Gothic restoration made according to the theories of Bülg. This portion is shown to men only. Behind the altar is a large and exceptionally inspiring mural of the Christian knight Donander, who fell in battle against the heathen, ascending to Heaven.

Château. —(Open 9 to 11.30 a.m. and 2 to 4 p.m. (from 1 October to Easter), 6 p.m. (Easter to 30 September). Admission:1F. There is also a Son et Lumière in summer, French 8.30, English 9.45 p.m. Admission: 1.50 F.)

Little remains of the stronghold of Dom Manuel, and nothing of his tomb, whose ornate monument was razed during the Revolution. The existing structure is mainly the work of Florian, fourth Duc de Puysange, restored according to Bülg, and looks about as one would expect. It houses a museum which includes some interesting relics (among them two balls said to have belonged to Jurgen the pawnbroker, an iridescent shirt of undoubted antiquity whose radioactivity cannot be accounted for, a chastity belt in pristine condition bearing the arms of Alianora of Provence, and a set of specifications for a solar system initialled "K") as well as an inexplicable collection of manuscripts and other scribblings by some obscure American writer.

The remnant of the original building is known as the Room of Ageus and contains three unusual windows.

Other Things to See

Pont de Duardenez. —This bridge over the river is a favorite spot for anglers, whose catches are occasionally of a unique variety of blind fish.

Hôtel Freydis. —Look into the courtyard of this somewhat peculiar inn for a sight of ten amusing small statues.

—Poul and Karen Anderson

ROBERT A. HEINLEIN

Guest of Honor, World Science Fiction
Convention, 1976

Your universe is ruled by common sense:
   Though on the road to glory Waldo saw
   Magic incorporate the Devil's law,
Your empire's logic holds by pounds and pence;

And though your misfits build a crooked house,
   Or by their bootstraps find the door to summer,
   Though double stardom trap a passing
   mummer,
Your roads will only roll where trade allows;

And men must sell the moon—lunch isn't free.
   If starship troopers march, and blowups come
   (Solutions with no satisfying sum)
Can citizenhood win the Galaxy?

   But fear no evil: for, these things above,
   Each life-line still binds time enough for love.

                —Karen Anderson

TREATY IN TARTESSOS

Iratzabal's hoofs were shod with bronze, as befitted a high chief, and heavy gold pins held the
coils of bright sorrel hair on top of his head. In
this morning's battle, of course, he had used
wooden pins which were less likely to slip out.
As tonight was a ceremonial occasion, he wore a
coat of aurochs hide dyed blue with woad, but-
toned and cinched with hammered gold.

He waved his spear high to show the green
branches bound to its head as he entered the
humans' camp. No one spoke, but a guard
grunted around a mouthful of barley-cake and
jerked his thumb toward the commander's tent.

Standing in his tent door, Kynthides eyed the
centaur with disfavor, from his unbarbered hair
to the particularly clumsy bandage on his off
fetlock. He straightened self-consciously in his
sea-purple cloak and pipeclayed linen tunic.

"Greetings, most noble Iratzabal," he said, bowing. "Will you enter my tent?"

The centaur returned the bow awkwardly. "Glad to, most noble Kynthides." he said. As he went in the man realized with a little surprise that the centaur emissary was only a couple of fingers' breadth taller than himself.

It was darker inside the tent than out, despite the luxury of three lamps burning at once. "I hope you've dined well? May I offer you anything?" Kynthides asked politely, with considerable misgivings. The centaur probably wouldn't know what to do with a barley loaf, and as for wine—well, there wasn't a drop within five miles of camp. Or there had better not be.

"That's decent of you, but I'm full up," said Iratzabal. "The boys found a couple of dead . . . uh, buffalo, after the battle, and we had a fine barbecue."

Kynthides winced. Another yoke of draft oxen gone! Well, Corn Mother willing, the war would be settled soon. It might even be tonight. "Won't you, er . . . Sit? Lie down? Er, make yourself comfortable."

Iratzabal lowered himself to the ground with his feet under him, and Kynthides sank gratefully into a leather-backed chair. He had been afraid the discussion would be conducted standing up.

"I got to admit you gave us a good fight today, for all you're such lightweights," the centaur said. "You generally do. If we don't get things settled somehow, we could go on like this till we've wiped each other out."

"We realize that too," said the man. "I've been asked by the heads of every village in Tartessos, not to mention communities all the way back to Thrace, to make some reasonable settlement with you. Can you speak for centaurs in those areas?"

"More or less." He swished his tail across the bandaged fetlock, and flies scattered. "I run most of the territory from here up through Goikokoa Etchea—what men call Pyrene's Mountains—and across to the Inland Sea. Half a dozen tribes besides mine hunt through here, but they stand aside for *us*. We could lick any two of them with our eyes shut. Now, you take an outfit like the Acroceraunians—I don't run them, but they've heard of me, and I can tell them to knuckle under or face my boys *and* yours. But that shouldn't be necessary. I'm going to get them a good cut."

"Well, remember that if the communities don't like promises I make in their names, they won't honor them," said the man. He slid his fingers through the combed curls of his dark-brown beard and wished he could ignore the centaur's odor. The fellow smelled like a saddle-blanket. If he didn't want to wash, he could at least use perfume. "First, we ought to consider the reasons for this war, and after that ways to settle the dispute."

"The way I see it," the centaur began, "is, you folks want to pin down the corners of a piece of country and sit on it. We don't understand ground belonging to somebody."

"It *began*," Kynthides said stiffly, "with that riot at the wedding."

"That was just what set things off," said Iratzabal. "There'd been a lot of small trouble before then. I remember how I was running down a four-pointer through an oak wood one rainy day, with my nose full of the way things smell when they're wet and my mind on haunch of venison. The next thing I knew I was in a clearing planted with one of those eating grasses, twenty pounds of mud on each hoof and a pack of tame wolves worrying my hocks. I had to kill two or three of them before I got away, and by then there were men throwing spears and shouting 'Out! Out!' in what they thought was Eskuara."

"We have to keep watchdogs and arm the field hands, or we wouldn't have a stalk of grain standing at harvest time!"

"Take it easy. I was just telling you, the war isn't over a little thing like some drunks breaking up a wedding. Nor they wouldn't have, if the wine hadn't been where they could get at it. There's blame on both sides."

The man half rose at this, but caught himself. The idea was to stop the war, not set it off afresh. "At any rate, it seems we can't get along with each other. Men and centaurs don't mix well."

"We look at things different ways, said Iratzabal. "You see a piece of open country, and all you can think of is planting a crop on it. We think of deer grazing it, or rabbit and pheasant nesting. Field-planting ruins the game in a district."

"Can't you hunt away from farm districts?" asked Kynthides. "We have our families to support, little babies and old people. There are too many of us to let the crops go and live by hunting, even if there were as much game as the land could support."

"Where can we hunt?" shrugged the centaur. "Whenever we come through one of our regular districts, we find more valleys under plow than last time, more trees cut and the fields higher up the slope. Even in Goikokoa Etchea, what's as much my tribe's home as a place can be, little fields are showing up." A swirl of lamp smoke veered toward him, and he sniffed it contemptuously. "Sheep fat! The herds I find aren't deer any more, they're sheep, with a boy pi-pipping away on a whistle—and dogs again."

"If you'd pick out your territory and stay on it, then no farmers would come in," said Kynthides. "It's contrary to our nature to leave land unused because somebody plans to hunt through it next autumn."

"But, big as Goikokoa Etchea is, it won't begin to feed us year round! We've got to have ten times as much, a hundred times if you're talking of Scythia and Illyria and all."

"I live in Thessaly myself," Kynthides pointed out. "I have to think of Illyria. What we men really want is to see all you centaurs completely out of Europe, resettled in Asia or the like. Couldn't you all move out of Sarmatia and the lands to the east? Nobody lives there. It's all empty steppes."

"Sarmatia! Maybe it looks empty to a farmer, but I've heard from the boys in Scythia. The place is filling up with Achaians, six feet tall, each with twenty horses big enough to eat either one of us for breakfast, and they can ride those horses all night and fight all day. By Jainco, I'm keeping away from them."

"Well, there's hardly anybody in Africa. Why don't you go there?" the man suggested.

"If there was any way of us all getting there—"

"Certainly there is! We have ships. It would take a couple of years to send you all, but—"

"*If* we could get there, we wouldn't like it at all. That's no kind of country for a centaur. Hot, dry, game few and far between—no thanks. But you're willing to ship us all to some other place?"

"Any place! That is, within reason. Name it."

"Just before war broke out in earnest, I got chummy with a lad who'd been on one of those exploring voyages you folks go in for. He said he'd been to a place that was full of game of all kinds, and even had the right kind of toadstools."

"Toadstools?" To make poison with?" cried Kynthides, his hand twitching toward the neatly bandaged spear-jab on his side."

"*Poison!*" Iratzabal ducked his head and laughed into his heavy sorrel beard." That's a good one, poison from toadstools! No, to eat. Get a glow on at the Moon Dances—same way you people do with wine. Though I can't see why you use stuff that leaves you so sick the next day."

"Once you've learned your capacity, you needn't have a hangover," Kynthides said with a feeling of superiority. "But this place you're talking of—"

"Well, my pal said it wasn't much use to men, but centaurs would like it. Lots of mountains, all full of little tilted meadows, but no flat country to speak of. Not good to plow up and sow with barely or what-not. Why not turn that over to us, since you can't send any big colonies there anyway?"

"Wait a minute. Are you talking about Kypros' last expedition?"

"That's the one my pal sailed under," nodded Iratzabal.

"No, by the Corn Mother! How can I turn that place over to you? We've barely had a look at it ourselves! There may be tin and amber to rival Thule, or pearls, or sea-purple. We have simply no idea of what we'd be giving you."

"And there may be no riches at all. Did this guy Kypros say he'd seen any tin or pearls? If he did, he didn't tell a soul of his crew. And I'm telling you, if we don't go there we don't go anyplace. I can start the war again with two words."

The man sprang to his feet, white-lipped. "Then start the war again! We may not have been winning, but by the Mother, we weren't losing!"

Iratazabal heaved himself upright. "You can hold out as long as we give you pitched battles. But wait till we turn to raiding! You'll have fields trampled every night, and snipers chipping at you every day. You won't dare go within bowshot of the woods. We'll chivy your herds through your crops till they've run all their fat off and there's not a blade still standing. And you'll get no harvest in, above what you grab off the stem and eat running. How are the granaries, Kynthides? Will there be any seed corn left by spring?"

The man dropped into his chair and took his head in trembling hands. "You've got us where we hurt. We can't survive that kind of warfare. But how can I promise land that isn't mine? It belongs to Kypros' backers, if anyone."

"Pay them off in the grain that won't be spoiled. Fix up the details any way it suits you. I'm not trying to make it hard on you—we can kick through with a reasonable number of pelts and such to even the bargain."

He looked up. "All right, Iratzabal," he said wearily. "You can *have* Atlantis."

—Karen Anderson

A PHILOSOPHICAL DIALOGUE

"Hey, a great idea for an essay!" exclaimed the lady. "A sure-fire attention-getter. Come out against God, motherhood, and apple pie, and in favor of sin and the man-eating shark."

"That's *new?*" answered the gentleman. "You must have a different angle—"

"I'll think of one. For instance, motherhood increases population pressure and the man-eating shark reduces it. Didn't you see George O.'s letter in *Analog?*"

"Yes. Really, though, darling, these days the position you want me to take is dismally conventional. Much more effective to declare in favor of God, motherhood, and apple pie, and against sin and the man-eating shark."

"Won't work. People would only say, 'That's him again, on his back-to-McKinley kick.'"

"You prefer Nixon? Having barely survived

246

Johnson and Kennedy? But anyhow, brighteyes, I'm well aware that these days it is not necessary and certainly not sufficient to argue from fact and logic. Your grounds must be fashionable."

"Okay, let's hear."

"Snuggle closer, hm? Now let me think— Ah, yes.

"God. Well, after all, without God there wouldn't be churches, would there? And without churches, there wouldn't be any Social Gospel or Fathers Berrigan and Groppi or many other delightful features of our mod world. And besides, you know, God is real groovy. Like in *Playboy* a little while back, remember, they had this article proving what a swinger Jesus was. And man has to find Meaning—he has to get away from Dehumanizing Science—and, sure, you can find Meaning if you say Om often enough, but you can find it in First Corinthians too; and Christianity draws from so many different religions that it has more to offer than its predecessors, whose temple rites, shamans, and gods were generally pretty brutal; in other words, Christianity can drive you a lot crazier than ziggurats and witches and vile, vile Rimmon.

"Next—don't bother me, I'm trying to think— motherhood. You must realize that the concept involves more than simply farrowing. The image of Mother requires a child already in the world—a whole family, in fact, of which she is the serene, benign, tender but infinitely strong and patient center—to which she devotes her entire life, considering herself happy if at the end when she is old, her children kiss her work-worn hands before they set her little grandchildren on her lap that she may cuddle and care for these too. . . . Yes. Let's by all means associate reproduction with motherhood; let's get this fixed in every female heart and soul. The population curve will nosedive!

"Apple pie. . . . Don't bother me, I said. . . . Well, if you want to bother me *that* way—

"Ah, yes. Apple pie. Good old-fashioned American apple pie. None of these frozen imitations, produced by impersonal machines in some atmosphere-polluting factory for the profit of greedy capitalists. No, people should do for themselves, expressing their individuality in arts and crafts and apple pies. In fact, they ought to raise their own apples—and wheat, which they can personally plant, harvest, thresh, and mill—thereby helping the environment, since green leaves revitalize the air. . . . And having baked several extra pies, you can trade them to your neighbor for some wool off the sheep he keeps, which you can wash, card, spin, and weave with your own individual hands."

The gentleman stopped for breath. "What about the negative side?" asked the lady. "You're supposed to be against—"

"Sin. I know," he replied. "The kinds of sin being legion, let's stay by the nineteenth-century equation of it with fornication, and see if we can convince enlightened modern youth of the virtue of chastity. Hm-m-m. . . .

"One doesn't ordinarily get positive results by saying, when first introduced to a girl, 'How do you do? Do you fornicate?' At least, I never did, though I admit being too chicken to try. A certain amount of courtship is involved. And even after they have bedded, a couple must find things to do outside of this, or the relationship will perish of boredom and thus the fornication will stop.

"Therefore sinning takes time that could better be spent in demonstrating, rioting, and other socially conscious activities. It induces people to buy gifts for each other, making more profits for the corrupt establishment. They tend to drive around in automobiles, befouling the atmosphere. The mechanical contraceptives they throw away are not very bio-degradable. Or, if they use pills, these are produced in factories whose effluents doubtless go into the rivers.

"Obviously, the only way to be with it nowadays is to stay celibate."

"Really?" she murmured.

"I am a hopeless reactionary," he reminded her.

"You haven't finished," she said. "You've still got the man-eating shark."

"Forget it. A shark is not what I want right now—oh, all right. Simple. If man-eating sharks are around, people avoid swimming. This has several bad effects. For one, they don't get close to nature in that particular fashion. Instead, they stay in town, going to a movie or drinking in a bar or otherwise helping support the corrupt establishment. Furthermore, if they don't swim, they're less aware of the extent to which the water is polluted, and thus less likely to get active in the struggle to save our environment. And finally, when a shark does eat a man, it converts him to ordure, and too much untreated human waste is already being dumped into the oceans.

"Are you satisfied?"

"Not yet," she said.

"Same here," he agreed. "Let's stop talking and develop a meaningful relationship."

"Can't we just have fun?" she asked.

—Poul Anderson

PROFESSOR JAMES

(melody: "Jesse James")

Moriarty was the name of brothers both called
James,
A colonel and a former math professor.
The prof went bad in time, and so he turned to
crime
The crafty brain of which he was possessor.

> (Chorus)   Moriarty in his time was Napo-
> leon of crime.
> He wanted not for ally nor for
> slave.
> But Sherlock was the guy who
> wouldn't drop or die,
> And he laid Moriarty in his grave.

Moriarty squatted and feloniously plotted
In the spiderweb of tangled London town.
A thread had but to twitch, and 'twould help to
make him rich;
He'd dream a scheme and sell it for cash
down.

When Sherlock crossed his path, he first with-
held his wrath.
But soon his plots were hampered absolutely.
He swore that he respected Holmes' style as he
detected—

He'd murder Holmes regretting it acutely.

He didn't offer payoff, but he did ask Holmes to
    lay off,
Explaining that he otherwise must die.
Sherlock said to him, "Although the prospect's
    grim,
At least we'll go together, you and I."

Now Moriarty swore he'd save his own dear
    gore,
And sent his hoods to fix an accident:
But Sherlock was too wary and he knew he
    shouldn't tarry,
So he dodged them all and toured the
    Continent.

The little fish were netted, the ones the prof
    abetted,
By evidence that Holmes sent Scotland Yard;
But the shark himself got free across the narrow
    sea
And hunted Holmes to catch him off his guard.

Moriarty found the track that led to
    Reichenbach
And by a trick got Sherlock all alone.
A note upon the brink was the end, as all did
    think,
Of the best and wisest man we've ever known.

The Final Problem's end had robbed us of our
    friend
And left a void that no one else could fill.

But his fire no man could douse, and in *The Empty House*
We found that Sherlock Holmes was with us still.

—Poul and Karen Anderson

LANDSCAPE WITH SPHINXES

The pride was a small one, even as sphinxes go. An arrogant black mane blew back over Arctanax's shoulders and his beard fluttered against his chest. Ahead and a little below soared Murrhona and Selissa, carrying the remnants of the morning's kill. It was time the cubs were weaned.

The valley lifted smooth and broad from the river, then leaped suddenly in sandstone cliffs where the shadows seemed more solid then the thorny, gray-green scrub. A shimmer of heat ran along wind-scoured edges.

In the tawny rocks about the eyrie, the cubs played at stalk-the-unicorn. They were big-eyed, dappled, and only half fledged. Taph, the boy, crept stealthily up a sun-hot slab, peeking around it from time to time to be sure that the moly blossom still nodded on the other side. He reached the top and shifted his feet excitedly. That moly was about to be a dead unicorn. The tip of his tail twitched at the thought.

His sister Fiantha forgot the blossom at once. Pounce! and his tail was caught between her paws; he rolled back down on top of her, all claws out. They scuffled across baked clay to the edge of a thornbush and backed apart.

Taph was about to attack again when he saw the grownups dip down from above. He leaped across Fiantha and bounded toward the cave mouth. She came a jump and a half behind. They couldn't kiss Murrhona and Selissa because of the meat in their jaws, so they kissed Father twice instead.

"Easy, there! Easy!" Arctanax coughed, but he was grinning. "Get back into the cave, the two of you. How often do I have to tell you to stay in the cave?" The cubs laughed and bounced inside.

Selissa dropped the meat she had been carrying and settled down to wash her face, but Murrhona called her cubs over to eat. She watched critically as they experimented with their milk-teeth on this unfamiliar substance.

"Hold it down with your paw, Fiantha," she directed. "If you just tug at it, it'll follow you all over the floor. Like Taph—No, Taph, use your side teeth. They're the biggest and sharpest." And so the lesson went. After a while both cubs got tired of the game and nuzzled for milk.

Selissa licked her right paw carefully and polished the bridge of her broad nose. There was still a trace of blood smell; she licked and polished again.

"You can't rush them," she said rather smugly. "I remember *my* first litter. Time and again I thought they'd learned a taste for meat, but even when they could kill for themselves—only conies and such, but their own kill—they still came back to suck."

"Oh, I remember how put out you were when you realized you still had to hold quiet for nursing," Murrhona smiled lazily. She licked down a tuft behind Fiantha's ear and resettled her wings. "But I really hate to see them grow up. They're so cute with their little spots."

Selissa shrugged and polished the bridge of her nose again for good measure. If you wanted to call them *cute*, with their wings all pinfeathers and down shedding everywhere—! Well, yes, she had to admit they were, in a way. She licked her paw once more, meditatively, put her chin down on it and dozed off.

An hour later Fiantha woke up. Everybody was asleep. She stretched her wings, rolled onto her back, and reached her paws as far as she could. The sun outside was dazzling. She rubbed the back of her head against the cool sandstone floor and closed her eyes, intending to go back to sleep, but her left wing itched. When she licked at it, the itch kept moving around, and bits of down came loose on her tongue.

She rolled over on her stomach, spat out the fluff, and licked again. There—*that* did it!

Fully awake now, she noticed the tip of Arctanax's tail and pounced.

"Scram," he muttered without really waking. She pounced again just as the tail-tip flicked out of reach. Once more and she had it, chewing joyously.

"Scram, I said!" he repeated with a cuff in her general direction. She went on chewing, and added a few kicks. Arctanax rolled over and bumped into Selissa, who jumped and gave Fiantha a swat in case she needed it. Fiantha mewed with surprise. Murrhona sprang up, brushing Taph aside; he woke too and made a dash for Selissa's twitching tail.

"Can't a person get *any* rest around here?" grumbled Arctanax. He heaved himself up and walked a few feet away from his by now well-tangled family.

"They're just playful," Murrhona murmured.

"If this is play, I'd hate to see a fight," said Selissa under her breath. She patted Taph away and he tumbled enthusiastically into a chewing match with Fiantha.

"Go to sleep, children," Murrhona suggested, stretching out again. "It's much too hot for games."

Fiantha rolled obediently away from Taph, and found a good place to curl up, but she wasn't the least bit sleepy. She leaned her chin on a stone and looked out over the valley. Down there, in the brown-roasted grass, something moved toward a low stony ridge.

There were several of them, and they didn't walk like waterbuck or unicorn; it was a queer, bobbing gait. They came slowly up the ridge and out of the grass. Now she could see them better. They had heads like sphinxes, but with skimpy little manes, and no wings at all; and— and—

"Father, *look!*" she squeaked in amazement. "What kind of animal is that?"

He got up to see. "I don't know," he replied. "Never saw anything like it in all my born days. But then, we've had a lot of queer creatures wandering in since the glaciers melted."

"Is it game?" asked Taph.

"Might be," Arctanax said. "But I don't know any game that moves around in the middle of the day like that. It isn't natural."

"And the funny way they walk, too," added Fiantha.

"If they're silly enough to walk around like that at mid-day," Arctanax said as he padded back to an extra-cool corner of the cave, "I'm not surprised they go on two legs."

—Karen Anderson

ALPHA, BETA

Not quite thirteen that famous August, I
Learned α, β, γ to compare
The blazing secrets troubled atoms share
With phoenix stars that die and burn and die.
I learned to spell with ξ and μ and π
Mesons cascading from the sills of space
In shower on crackling shower at frantic pace
Where vacuum softens to electric sky.

Strange when I learned, one winter through, to
   spell
With those same symbols in their first design;
Haltingly sound out particle and ray,
And read past protons ancient tales that tell
How heroes praised strong gods and drank strong
   wine,
And, singing, hoisted sail for Troy one day.

                —Karen Anderson

A BLESSEDNESS OF SAINTS

Some years ago, the University of California library had an exhibit of old maps. Colorful things. Modern charts don't compare. Coordinate grids make a drab substitute for wind gods going oompa, oompa, and contour lines are no fair exchange at all for the actual contours on some of those mermaids. To hell with radicals like Goldwater—let's bring back the *eighteenth* century! But I digress. What I started out to mention was a Spanish map of the western hemisphere, dated 17something and not very detailed. One place they did show was Cape Canaveral. And out in the Pacific they had, neatly labeled, the Islas de San Dwich.

When Anthony Boucher heard about this, he laughed and said that must be a Catalan saint. It's tempting to develop the hagiography further . . . Dwich, apostle to the Anthropophagi, martyred by being sliced very thin and served on rye bread with mustard ... he did persuade the cannibals to postpone his execution twenty-four hours, till Saturday ... But this moving tale had better not be written. There are far too many spurious saints already.

Some of them are etymological too, like that St. Sophia to whom the cathedral in Constantinople was not dedicated. (For the benefit of any barbarians in my audience, though surely there are none, "Hagia Sophia" means "Holy Wisdom.") I've also heard of St. Trinity (Hagia Triada), St. Saviour, and a St. Cross believed to have been a Frenchman. James Branch Cabell mentions a St. Undecimilla whose name gave rise to the legend of the eleven thousand virgins—for whom, by the way, the Virgin Islands were named—and say, couldn't a martini be called a vergin?—But I'm digressing again.

A vast number of saints got into the calendar during the Dark and Middle Ages, before canonization had become a controlled procedure. Some were historical enough, though their claims to sainthood are, to put it politely, arguable. St. Olaf of Norway is still accepted, but even in medieval times people admitted that he didn't attain any state of grace till rather late in life. One of my ambitions is to go onto the campus of St. Olaf College, a strait-laced Lutheran institution in my home town, barricade myself on the water tower, and through a bullhorn read aloud some of the racier passages from the original chronicles of the patron—murders, robberies, booze hoistings, illegitimate son, and all.

Charlemagne was canonized by an anti-Pope at the request of Frederick Barbarossa; his festival was celebrated in some parts till fairly recently. The Byzantine Empress Zoe, whose career would have made Theodora blush, is a saint in the Eastern church though naturally not among the Romans: likewise Alexander Nevsky, because he stopped a bunch of Catholic invaders. In late years the Vatican has been re-examining the credentials of its saints and has dropped a lot of them, especially the fictitious ones. St. Hippolytus, for instance, who was said to have been dragged to death by horses, is merely Theseus' son from pagan Greek legend. St. Philomena has likewise been declared to be fabulous. I mean fabulous in the original sense of the word. The modern sense could be applied to the legendary St. Mary the Egyptian, a pilgrim to the Holy Land who worked out her passage in an interesting capacity.

However, no right-thinking Anglophile can go along with this business of demoting St. George to apocryphal status. Impossible. Utter nonsense. St. George doubtful? Gad, sir, that sort of thing just isn't said. Least of all where the servants might overhear. Shows you how schism is bound to turn into sheer heresy, by Jove. Ever since those Romans left the C. of E. . . . St. George for merrie England! God send the right! Death to the French! But first a pint at the George and Dragon. . . .

One perfectly genuine saint often confuses people. The Scandinavians have an ancient custom of lighting bonfires on Midsummer Eve; but who's this here Sankt Hans they talk about?

Getting back to fictional ones, though, it's surprising how many purely literary instances I can think of offhand. Norman Douglas' *South Wind* has a St. Dodecanus who—even in the probability-world of the novel—looks implausible. Karen tells me there's a St. Katy the Virgin who was a pig (again using the word in its original sense) but she can't remember any details. There is certainly a pig that goes to Heaven in *Der Heilige Antonius von Padua*, Wilhelm Busch's hilarious parody of the medieval Lives of the Saints. (He also originated the Katzenjammer Kids, way back in the last century; they were Max und Moritz then.) Science fiction fandom has an Order of St. Fantony. The most famous hallows in science fiction itself are surely Boucher's Aquin—though here again you're left in doubt whether the sanctity is real—and Miller's Leibowitz. Fritz Leiber's robots in *The Silver Eggheads* have a cult of saints with names like Karel and Isaac.

Not all are so pleasant. I once described an accursed church of St. Grimmin's-in-the-Wold, and a sonnet by H.P. Lovecraft warns you: "Beware St. Toad's cracked chimes." But of course the ultimately sinister figure in this subclass of dubiously benevolent imaginary saints is Trinian.

Some names lead me to wonder about their possible calendrical origin. Who was the St. Peter (Ste. Pierre) Smirnoff whose name adorns vodka bottles? Any killjoys who claim that "Ste."

stands for "Société" and is a feminine form anyway, will please take their business elsewhere. I want to believe in some good, kind, white-bearded holy man who passed the miracle of turning water into vodka. Does St. Exupéry derive from a Christian named Exuperius, whom Nero martyred by shooting him from a catapult? St. Gaudens and St. Saëns likewise revive a flagging sense of wonder.

There are millions of St. Johns. About forty years back, a Robert St. John was a well-known journalist and radio personality. He was also bearded, long before this was fashionable. The story goes that once he was waiting for a friend in a hotel lobby. A stranger came up and asked who he was. "I am St. John," he replied, a bit miffed at not being recognized. "Ah," said the stranger, "here for the Baptist convention, I suppose?"—I shall always think of him as St. John the Commentator.

Who is not to be confused with St. John the Persian, a writer of poems, or with that Burroughs illustrator, the late J. Allen, who is surely St. John of Barsoom.

The title of saint has sometimes been humorously bestowed, notably on Simon Templar. I'll close this piece with an anecdote which probably no one but Minnesotans and the omniscient Avram Davidson will appreciate. Years ago, the state university there had a physics professor named Anthony Zeleny, a very moral man who gave little lectures on the evils of smoking and drinking, in between differential equations. Now the tech students at Minnesota have an annual day of parades, ceremonies, and frolic, presided over by St. Patrick, the patron of engineers. (When he chased the snakes from Ireland, he invented the worm drive.) So one year a float came along bearing an enormous caricature statue of Professor Zeleny, cigarette in one hand, whisky bottle in the other, and gorgeous blonde on his knee. The float was labelled "St. Anthony Falls."

—Poul Anderson

ORIGIN OF THE SPECIES

I can see it now: they were ready to lift gravs
(Or whatever they did) but the cats weren't in
the ship.
"Here, kitty!" they called, in whatever outland-
ish way
They spoke to cats; but the cats were out in the
sun
Rolling about and sparring, and didn't come.
They held the airlock open, with tentacles
Or claws or something, that clenched impatiently
(I know how they felt) but the cats still wouldn't
come.
And then they tried to catch them; well, what
good
Has that ever done, when cats don't feel like
coming?
The cats scampered off, flicking their tails in
the air,
And all climbed up in some trees; and there
they sat
Sneeringly patient. Nothing could be done—
It was time to leave—they put it in the log,
"Third planet of Athfan's Star: the cats deserted."

—Karen Anderson

CONJUNCTION

(Venus and Jupiter, February 1975)

How pale is Venus in the lingering light
  When sun is set, but day is not yet done;
While in the thronging lights of middle night
  Great Jupiter has splendor matched by none.

But watch them now, as in the western sky
  Along the paths for them aforetime set
He night by night strides lower, she more high,
  Until the stars of Power and Love are met.

Behold, as night around them darkens, how
  Queen Venus' glory overmasters Jove,
Nor doubt the truth of what we witness now
  On earth below as in the skies above:
For as each subject to the king must bow
  So even kings must bow them down to Love.

—Karen Anderson

ADONIS RECOVERED. The asteroid 1936 CA Adonis, missing for 41 years, has now been recovered. —*Sky and Telescope*, April 1977.

ADONIS RECOVERED

We first beheld him twoscore years ago,
   Poor fleeting pebble, named and straightway lost
   Amidst the myriads of the starry host
Whose birth and death and life we seek to know;
Among the worlds of nobler state and show
   How briefly seen was faint Adonis' light
   Ere he receded into Stygian night,
Thenceforth to come unsought, unseen to go.

Unseen, but not forgotten: we but wait
   Until we have the means to find our strays:
   As with Adonis, Venus' wandering lover,
Lost asteroids anew we calculate,
   And comets long perturbed to distant ways
     We still remember, hoping to recover.

—Karen Anderson

THE PIEBALD HIPPOGRIFF

The edge of the world is fenced off stoutly enough, but the fence isn't made that will stop a boy. Johnny tossed his pack and coil of rope over it and started climbing. The top three strands were barbed wire. He caught his shirt as he went over, and had to stop for a moment to ease himself off. Then he dropped lightly to the grass on the other side.

The pack had landed in a clump of white clover. A cloud of disturbed bees hung above, and he snatched it away quickly lest they should notice the honeycomb inside.

For a minute he stood still, looking out over the edge. This was different from looking through the fence, and when he moved it was slowly. He eased himself to the ground where a corner of rock rose clear of the thick larkspur and lay on his belly, the stone hard and cool under his chin, and looked down.

The granite cliff curved away out of sight, and he couldn't see if it had a foot. He saw only endless blue, beyond, below, and on both sides. Clouds passed slowly.

Directly beneath him there was a ledge covered with long grass where clusters of stars bloomed on tall, slender stalks.

He uncoiled his rope and found a stout beech tree not too close to the edge. Doubling the rope around the bole, he tied one end around his waist, slung the pack on his back, and belayed himself down the cliff. Pebbles clattered, saxifrage brushed his arms and tickled his ears; once he groped for a hold with his face in a patch of rustling ferns.

The climb was hard, but not too much. Less than half an hour later he was stretched out on the grass with stars nodding about him. They had a sharp, gingery smell. He lay in the cool shadow of the world's edge for a while, eating apples and honeycomb from his pack. When he was finished he licked the honey off his fingers and threw the apple cores over, watching them fall into the blue.

Little islands floated along, rocking gently in air eddies. Sunlight flashed on glossy leaves of bushes growing there. When an island drifted into the shadow of the cliff, the blossoming stars shone out. Beyond the shadows, deep in the light-filled gulf, he saw the hippogriffs at play.

There were dozens of them, frisking and cavorting in the air. He gazed at them full of wonder. They pretended to fight, stooped at one another, soared off in long spirals to stoop and soar and stoop again. One flashed by him, a golden palomino that shone like polished wood. The wind whistled in its wings.

Away to the left, the cliff fell back in a wide crescent, and nearly opposite him a river tumbled over the edge. A pool on a ledge beneath caught most of the water, and there were hippogriffs drinking. One side of the broad pool was notched. The overflow fell sheer in a white plume blown sideways by the wind.

As the sun grew hotter, the hippogriffs began to settle and browse on the islands that floated past. Not far below, he noticed, a dozen or so stood drowsily on an island that was floating through the cliff's shadow toward his ledge. It would pass directly below him.

With a sudden resolution, Johnny jerked his rope down from the tree above and tied the end to a projecting knob on the cliff. Slinging on his pack again, he slid over the edge and down the rope.

The island was already passing. The end of the rope trailed through the grass. He slithered down and cut a piece off his line.

It was barely long enough after he had tied a noose in the end. He looked around at the hippogriffs. They had shied away when he dropped onto the island, but now they stood still, watching him warily.

Johnny started to take an apple out of his

pack, then changed his mind and took a piece of honeycomb. He broke off one corner and tossed it toward them. They fluttered their wings and backed off a few steps, then stood still again.

Johnny sat down to wait. They were mostly chestnuts and blacks, and some had white stockings. One was piebald. That was the one which, after a while, began edging closer to where the honeycomb had fallen. Johnny sat very still.

The piebald sniffed at the honeycomb, then jerked up its head to watch him suspiciously. He didn't move. After a moment it took the honeycomb.

When he threw another bit, the piebald hippogriff wheeled away, but returned almost at once and ate it. Johnny tossed a third piece only a few yards from where he was sitting.

It was bigger than the others, and the hippogriff had to bite it in two. When the hippogriff bent its head to take the rest Johnny was on his feet instantly, swinging his lariat. He dropped the noose over the hippogriff's head. For a moment the animal was too startled to do anything; then Johnny was on its back, clinging tight.

The piebald hippogriff leaped into the air, and Johnny clamped his legs about convulsed muscles. Pinions whipped against his knees and wind blasted his eyes. The world tilted; they were rushing downward. His knees pressed the sockets of the enormous wings.

The distant ramparts of the world swung madly, and he seemed to fall upward, away from the sun that suddenly glared under the hippogriff's talons. He forced his knees under the roots of the beating wings and dug heels into prickling hair. A sob caught his breath and he clenched his teeth.

The universe righted itself about him for a moment and he pulled breath into his lungs. Then they plunged again. Wind searched under his shirt. Once he looked down. After that he kept his eyes on the flutter of the feather-mane.

A jolt sent him sliding backward. He clutched the rope with slippery fingers. The wings missed a beat and the hippogriff shook its head as the rope momentarily checked its breath. It tried to fly straight up, lost way, and fell stiff-winged. The long muscles stretched under him as it arched its back, then bunched when it kicked straight out behind. The violence loosened his knees and he trembled with fatigue, but he wound the rope around his wrists and pressed his forehead against whitened knuckles. Another kick, and another. Johnny dragged at the rope.

The tense wings flailed, caught air, and brought the hippogriff upright again. The rope slackened and he heard huge gasps. Sunlight was hot on him again and a drop of sweat crawled down his temple. It tickled. He loosened one hand to dab at the annoyance. A new twist sent him sliding and he grabbed the rope. The tickle continued until he nearly screamed. He no longer dared let go. Another tickle developed beside the first. He scrubbed his face against the coarse fibre of the rope; the relief was like a world conquered.

Then they glided in a steady spiral that carried them upward with scarcely a feather's motion. When the next plunge came Johnny was ready for it and leaned back until the hippogriff arched its neck, trying to free itself from the pressure on its windpipe. Half choked, it glided again, and Johnny gave it breath.

They landed on one of the little islands. The hippogriff drooped its head and wings, trembling.

He took another piece of honeycomb from his pack and tossed it to the ground where the hippogriff could reach it easily. While it ate he stroked it and talked to it. When he dismounted the hippogriff took honeycomb from his hand. He stroked its neck, breathing the sweet warm feathery smell, and laughed aloud when it snuffled the back of his neck.

Tying the rope into a sort of hackamore, he mounted again and rode the hippogriff to the pool below the thunder and cold spray of the waterfall. He took care that it did not drink too much. When he ate some apples for his lunch, the hippogriff ate the cores.

Afterward he rode to one of the drifting islands and let his mount graze. For a while he kept by its side, making much of it. With his fingers, he combed out the soft flowing plumes of its mane, and examined its hoofs and the sickle-like talons of the forelegs. He saw how the smooth feathers on its forequarters became finer and finer until he could scarcely see where the hair on the hindquarters began. Delicate feathers covered its head.

The island glided further and further away

from the cliffs, and he watched the waterfall dwindle away to a streak and disappear. After a while he fell asleep.

He woke with a start, suddenly cold: the setting sun was below his island. The feathery odor was still on his hands. He looked around for the hippogriff and saw it sniffing at his pack.

When it saw him move, it trotted up to him with an expectant air. He threw his arms about the great flat-muscled neck and pressed his face against the warm feathers, with a faint sense of embarrassment at feeling tears in his eyes.

"Good old Patch," he said, and got his pack. He shared the last piece of honeycomb with his hippogriff and watched the sun sink still further. The clouds were turning red.

"Let's go see those clouds," Johnny said. He mounted the piebald hippogriff and they flew off, up through the golden air to the sunset clouds. There they stopped and Johnny dismounted on the highest cloud of all, stood there as it turned slowly gray, and looked into dimming depths. When he turned to look at the world, he saw only a wide smudge of darkness spread in the distance.

The cloud they were standing on turned silver. Johnny glanced up and saw the moon, a crescent shore far above.

He ate an apple and gave one to his hippogriff. While he chewed he gazed back at the world. When he finished his apple, he was about to toss the core to the hippogriff, but stopped himself and carefully took out the seeds first. With the seeds in his pocket, he mounted again.

He took a deep breath. "Come on, Patch," he said. "Let's homestead the moon."

—Karen Anderson

THE COASTS OF FAERIE

Minna was a child of the fisher folk who dwell by the narrow harbor of Noyo on the western sea. Every morning she went with her father into his boat, for no sons remained to him, to draw the ling cod from the cold salt-stinging water. Whether in sun or cloud or rain, each day they went forth; and whatever the weather near shore, there was always a bank of low-lying mist that retreated toward the horizon when they approached it.

One day as they returned to the narrow harbor Minna was sitting in the stern of the boat. She had taken the last fish from the hooks and coiled the lines. Now she looked behind, and saw that the mist was become clean-edged and had taken on the shape of hills like those of the land she knew.

"Look, Father!" she cried. "What land is that?"

"It is only the mist," said her father without turning, for the wind gusted about the bluffs and the harbor was not easy to enter.

"But look! There are hills afire with scarlet flowers!"

"It is only the sunset," said her father. They passed under the headland, and the sight was gone; and at the wharf the fish must be unloaded for the fish market, to be sold to the folk who lived in the town atop the bluff.

Many a time did Minna see that coastline as they returned with their fish to the harbor of Noyo, but her father would never look. "See to the lines," he would say. "It is only the mist." And Minna learned not to speak of it, but she watched. Not twice alike was the line of the hills, and the burning flowers changed their seeming as she watched: now poppies, now roses, now lilacs and purple heather. By this Minna understood that it was Faerie she saw. She looked, as if trying to will herself there: across the dark bitter water of the fishing grounds, to the silver shallows under the long lines of the hills, to the blossoming colors of the ridges. But her father bade her see to her work; and so she coiled the line. Its heavy hooks caught at her hands and left scratches that burned from the salt water.

When they came home, she would wash away the salt and salve the scratches, but they would scab and break open again the next day. And each night she went to her bed in the little room under the roof, and she dreamed of the hills of flowers, where youths and maidens wore robes of changing colors and danced a long dance along changing slopes and ridges. And every day was the same as every other, as they took the boat from the gray wharf and out of the narrow harbor and set the bait on the barbs of the hooks.

Out of the west one evening came a wind that smelled of roses and cinnamon, and on it were drifts of petals. "Look! Oh, look!" Minna cried; but her father would not look. She held up her hands and caught at the glowing petals, but when they touched her salt-burnt hands and the salt-crusted deck they vanished.

Minna gazed astern. Never had she seen those bright hills so close. Little wonder that the petals flew and the scent of flowers rode over the sea! The coast was so close that it almost seemed she might swim to it. As she gazed, she saw a gray dolphin frolicking in the wake.

"Oh, Dolphin!" Minna whispered, that her father might not hear. "Have you seen the shores of flowers?"

The dolphin nodded and dived and shot underwater to the stern of the boat. As he surfaced, he stood on his tail in the water and winked at her with his round bright eye. "Chipwheetwirl!" he called out, and Minna knew that it was his name.

"How far is it?" whispered Minna. "Can you carry me there, Chipwheetwirl?"

The dolphin nodded again and pointed his head toward the shifting shores. Minna understood. She threw off her heavy blue jacket, coarse trousers, and boots, and flung herself cleanly into the water. Its chill was a shock. She gasped as she came to the surface and stroked out after the dolphin.

The gray swell lifted heavily and slid her down into the trough. She swam steadily, but the cold sea pulled the strength from her limbs. A glance over her shoulder showed the boat small in the distance, but the blossoming hills seemed no closer. How much longer could she swim? She began to be frightened, and her stroke faltered.

"Chipwheetwirl!" she called. In moments he was beside her, rubbing her side and whistling encouragement.

"Can you help me?" she asked. She stretched out her arm and grasped at the dolphin's back. With a gurgle, he dived and came up on her other side, again playfully rubbing her.

"I can't play! I'm getting too tired to swim! Won't you help me?" she pleaded. The fear of the endless deep sank into her.

Chipwheetwirl gurgled again, and slipped beneath her so she could ride astride his back. As he carried her, he whistled and clicked at length. The meaning came to her in his tone: he had forgotten how weak her kind were, and apologized for not understanding sooner that she needed to be carried. He would take her to the shore as quickly as he could.

They were coming closer, and the petal-filled breeze came again, warm and full of spices. Suddenly they were past the first headland, and now the water too was warm, running silver and sweet over her legs. Vigor flowed into her veins. She had left the ocean her father fished and entered immortal waters. The bay was full of swimming folk and leaping dolphins. With a cry of delight, she slipped from Chipwheetwirl's back, and the scars and salt-burns washed away from her hands. The wavelet that lapped her cheek was silken. She laughed and frolicked with the pearl-shining dolphin, and swam on to the strand.

Youths and maidens swam beside her, splendid in their ivory-pale bodies, and they came to the shore together. "Welcome! Welcome to Minna the dreamer!" they called, and their speech was song. On the shell-white shore, they welcomed her with kisses and caresses. They clothed her like themselves in robes of cloth-of-blossom and brought her to trees of ambrosial fruit and chalice-flowers flowing with nectar. When she had eaten and drunk, Minna joined them in the long dance that is danced through the sunset bloom upon the shifting ridges.

In the narrow harbor of Noyo, the fisher folk went into their white wooden church to inform their god that he had had the right to take

Minna from them. And they tolled the bell in token that this was true.

But the sound of the bell did not reach Minna where she dwelt in joy on the ever-changing shores of the Vespern Empery.

—Karen Anderson

SHANIDAR IV

The discovery of pollen clusters of different flowers in the grave of one of the Neanderthals, No. IV, at Shanidar cave, Iraq, furthers our acceptance of the Neanderthals in our line of evolution. It suggests that, although the body was archaic, the spirit was modern.

—Ralph Solecki, "Shanidar IV, A Neanderthal Flower Burial in Northern Iraq," *Science*, vol.190, p. 880, 25 November 1975

Lay on his grave a springy bed of horsetail—
Over him scatter blooms of pungent yarrow,
As if that healing herb might heal his death;
Blue cornflower strew, and clustered purple drops

Of the grape hyacinth; pluck yellow suns
From thistles which spread wide the longest
days,
And with them sheafs of groundsel many-starred;
Bring in across the summer mountainside
From where each grows to solitary height
Rose-mallows bearing flowers as bright as blood.
Heap on him all that's fair, our love to mark,
Ere we heap earth and leave him in the dark.

—Karen Anderson